Acts of Love

Cameron Hart

Published by Cameron Hart, 2024.

ACTS OF LOVE

First edition. June 27, 2024.

Copyright © 2024 Cameron Hart.

ISBN: 979-8227891723

Written by Cameron Hart.

Want a free book?

Sign up for my newsletter[1] and get your free copy of Chasing Stacy!

One look at the stunning waitress carrying the weight of the world on her shoulders, and I'm a goner. I wasn't looking for a sweet little thing with auburn hair and more baggage than I can fit on the back of my bike, but there's no going back now. She's mine. I'll prove to her I'm more than capable of handling her past and making her feel safe again.

---

1. https://dl.bookfunnel.com/7wbqvhsx8r

Chapter 1

Weston

"Mr. Haze, if you would just—"

"No," I growl, pacing back and forth in my agent's office.

"But—"

"I said no. No way in hell am I going to fly out to Seattle to be in a community theater play." I stop pacing momentarily, just long enough to glare at Matthew and Linda, the two hard-asses on my PR team.

"Weston," my agent, Ted, says more calmly. "This is serious. You've had a string of... *incidents* lately and this last one..."

"Wasn't my fault!" I finish for him. "How many times do I have to explain it? Teresa was the one who caused the scene. She went in there looking to stir up drama. I told her to go away."

"No, you told her to fuck off," Linda unhelpfully adds. I shrug, not sure why that detail is important. The sentiment is the same either way. "You said it loudly, in a crowded Broadway theater on opening night. You also very publicly insulted her latest album."

I try, unsuccessfully, to hide my smirk. I didn't even listen to her last album, but I'm sure it was terrible. She had decent music once, but that was at least five years and four albums ago. Teresa Marie sold her soul to the almighty dollar, just like everyone else around here. Just like... me.

I shake my head of those thoughts, forcing myself not to feel the sharp sting of hypocrisy in my gut. I can't deal with an existential crisis right now. Not when I already have a PR crisis on my hands.

"She tried to slap me, for fuck's sake. How is that my fault?"

"And what about the guy you punched? Was that her fault, too?" Linda mutters.

"Yes," I groan, scrubbing my hands down my face. "If I wasn't trying to avoid her attack I never would have bumped into that guy. How was I supposed to know he was a Russian diplomat who had a security team around him? Someone grabbed me, so I threw a punch!"

Linda sighs defeatedly and shakes her head, leaning back in her seat.

"You were drunk," Matthew pipes in, trying to tackle this from a different angle. Between him and Linda, I know this is a losing battle, but I'm not giving up yet.

"I had a few drinks at intermission, but I wasn't drunk."

"Does it matter? The photos are damning. Your fist is cocked back for the punch while security holds you back. Teresa is in tears behind you, looking like she's trying to stop you. Even you have to admit that it looks bad."

"Alright, alright," Ted says, trying to diffuse the situation. "Let's not blow this up into something it's not."

I nod my head and motion toward my agent, letting my PR team know we should listen to him. He's strict but fair. One of the most well respected agents in the business. I was lucky enough to get picked up by him right after my first gig. I guess that pretty much summarizes my whole acting career—luck.

I was out working a construction job with a friend when some middle-aged lady stopped on the sidewalk and handed us her card, saying we should audition for an action film being shot a few blocks away on one of the beaches here in LA.

My buddy, Rider, and I thought she was giving us shit. Honestly, we thought it was some sort of reverse-construction-worker-catcall moment. But the lady just shrugged and said we could make a hell of a lot more than we were making in construction. Rider told her to scram, and that he wouldn't be caught dead waxing himself for a camera.

I wasn't so quick to dismiss the opportunity, however. At nineteen, money talked. At thirty-three, money still talks. The only other soul who knows about my humble beginnings, aside from Rider and the lady who gave me her business card, is Ted.

"We're not the ones blowing anything up," Linda says, her nasally, unpleasant voice piercing through my thoughts. "Mr. Haze, you hired us to rehab your public image after the beach house fiasco, and I must say, it's been a... challenge."

"That was hardly a *fiasco*, Linda. It was a party that got a little out of control."

"You set a boat on fire."

"No one was in it!" I protest. "And I bought the dude a way nicer boat. He wasn't even that mad about it."

"Then there's the speeding tickets—"

"Everyone gets speeding tickets."

"And showing up drunk for your latest movie premiere," Linda continues, ignoring my protests. "Flipping off the press, stealing food from a Michelin star restaurant, and now ruining the opening night of a highly anticipated Broadway play." She finishes her list of grievances and crosses her arms, staring at me like a disappointed mother.

"First of all, if you think I was the only person to show up drunk to that premiere, you're dead wrong. Secondly, that damn photographer had it coming. I should have done a lot more than flip him off. And usually, La Comptoir doesn't make me pay for my meal. How was I supposed to know the rules changed? Finally, for the last goddamn time, *the theater incident wasn't my fault.*"

"Well, that's not what ninety-nine percent of the public thinks," Matthew says. "At the end of the day, that's what matters."

The room is silent for the first time since this meeting started thirty minutes ago. I glance over at Ted, who gives me a slight nod of his head. He's letting me know this is the right choice, even though he's not thrilled about the plan, either.

I take a deep breath and roll my shoulders before plopping down in the nearest leather office chair.

"Okay. So, about this play," I say, looking to Linda. I hate the smug smile on her face, but she's right. I pay a lot of money for her PR firm to do a job, and they're doing it.

"It's not as bad as it sounds," she starts, shuffling through some papers. "Paramount Arts Theater in Seattle is an undiscovered gem. The director of this play is rather... *particular*, but he's excited to work with you." She hands me a script titled *No Stronger Love*.

"Please don't tell me this is some rom-com bullshit play," I groan, rubbing my temples.

"It's heavy on the romance, but it's no rom-com. You'll be Luther Calson, the leading role, for the limited debut showing. The play only runs for a week, which makes it perfect to slip right into your schedule," Linda rambles on.

I flip through the script and groan again when I read the character description. "I'm some lovestruck sap? Are you kidding me? I knew you wanted to give my public image a makeover, but no one is going to believe this shit."

"The best part is, no one knows you're in it," Matthew says, ignoring my protests once again.

"Shocker. I didn't even know until half an hour ago," I mutter.

"What I'm saying," he continues, giving me an annoyed look, "is that you'll be able to fly under the radar while in Seattle. Or at least that's the goal. Stay out of trouble, keep your head down, and blow everyone away with your performance. Boosting sales and recognition for a small play will show people you care about the arts—both theater and otherwise."

"Seems like a real win-win," I say bitterly.

"Exactly," Linda says. "I'm glad you're finally seeing things our way. Especially since you're boarding a plane in two hours."

"Excuse me?" I stand up, glaring at everyone in the room, including Ted. He at least has the decency to look shamed. The traitor. He knew all along.

"I really think this is the right move, Weston," Ted says quietly. He's a tall, broad man with a shock of white hair to go along with his full white beard. Ted rests his hands over his slight beer belly and shakes his head at me. "Ever since Teresa…"

"This isn't about Teresa," I grunt. It really isn't. She was vapid and horrible, and it was a huge relief when we finally ended things a year and a half ago. I didn't know how toxic my life had become until we broke up. These last eighteen months have admittedly been wild, and not necessarily in a good way. But it's not because of Teresa.

It's because… well, I can't quite say. I'm restless. Unsettled. Unsatisfied. I wake up with an ache in my chest, but I'm not sure why. I can't make myself go there. Not yet. If I tear away the money, fame, parties, and perks, what do I have left? Me. The thing is, I don't even know who I am anymore.

"It's settled then!" Linda says enthusiastically, clapping her hands. "Be sure to pack your raincoat. I hear Seattle has great weather this time of year."

***

"Ready for the next one? Then we can take a break. Talk shop. Maybe grab a drink?" Reggie Fields, the too-eager director leans in close as if we're trading secrets. We're not.

I scowl at him and sit back in my seat, taking another sip of coffee while silently cursing Ted, Matthew, and Linda. They failed to mention I'd be here for auditions, and even worse, that I'd be helping with casting. Each performance for the female lead is more cringeworthy than the last, and I'm guessing part of it is because of me. They weren't expecting a movie star to be here, but when they see me, they either turn into fangirls or pull down their necklines to show more cleavage.

"Let's get this over with," I mutter. I swear if I see one more bubbly bottle blonde gasp and gush over me being here, while tripping all over her lines and fake compliments, I'm quitting. Okay, I can't quit, but I'll…I don't know. Do *something*.

How did it come to this? How do I get my life back? Do I even want my life back?

Shit. Can't be thinking like that, and definitely not while I'm in public. I need a distraction, but there's no sports car to drive off in, or party to crash. Not that I need those things to be happy. If I'm being honest, I can't remember the last time I was happy. Not even happy, just... content. What does that feel like? Have I ever truly been content?

Whatever.

I swallow down the unwelcome, but not unfamiliar feelings of doubt and dread, and let my eyes wander around the small space. It's old, but not dirty. Small, but not cramped. The stage left stairs could use some work, but...

Who is that?

Standing off to the left of the stage, slightly hidden behind a curtain, is the most precious woman I've ever seen. I don't think I've ever used that word to describe someone, but nothing else fits the little ray of sunshine standing twenty feet away from me.

Her bright, white-blonde hair shimmers in the spotlight as it's swung around to point toward center stage. There's no way that came from a bottle. It's so light and ethereal, I'm nearly blinded by the way it sparkles.

The angel tucks a strand of her beautiful hair behind her ear and then smooths out a few wrinkles on her white blouse. That's another thing that stands out. She's in a white button up blouse and formfitting black slacks. Is that a cardigan folded over her arm? Adorable. She looks like she's going to work in an accounting office, not about to audition for a leading role.

Seriously, who is this woman? I can't take my eyes off her. She looks down at her hands, which I can clearly see are shaking. She balls them up into fists, takes a deep breath in, then exhales all of the tension in her body.

And Jesus, what a body she has. Even in the conservative getup, I can see she's sweet, curvy perfection. Why is her starched appearance such a turn on? I want to glide my hands up and down her sides, kneading the soft flesh of her hips, her ass... God, I want to peel off her shirt and see what's hiding underneath. Is she wearing a matching bra and panty set? Are they lacey little things? I can think of at least a dozen ways I could relieve her tension.

But it's more than lust. Other thoughts flood my mind, confusing thoughts about taking care of her. I have the urge to wrap her up in a blanket and hold her close while I kiss her cute little nose. What the hell is that all about? I want to hug her as much as I want to fuck her.

Dammit. I can't think like that. I'm not here for a woman. I'm pretty sure Linda would kill me with her bare hands if I hooked up with my costar. I might not have to worry about that, however. From the looks of it, the girl is about two seconds away from bolting. I see her eye the door to the lobby, and then the emergency exit behind her, before staring at her hands again.

Stay, I silently encourage her. Why, I have no idea, but it's suddenly imperative that she audition for this role. I have to know more about her. What brought this angel here? Why is she so anxious? And most importantly, what is she doing to me?

I'm somehow both on edge and calm. Being in her presence and seeing her sunshine soothes the gnawing ache in my chest. Yet knowing she's so nervous, so flighty, so fucking gorgeous, has me fidgeting in my seat. She can't just leave. She's the first flicker of light I've seen in so damn long. Maybe ever. I didn't know how dark my life was until this moment.

She squares her shoulders, lifts her head, and opens her eyes. Suddenly, I relate to my lovestruck sap role in a deep, visceral way. Well, fuck. Looks like Linda is going to kill me.

Chapter 2

Shay

"You can do this, you can do this, you can do this," I mutter to myself as I walk onto the stage to audition for the part of Seneca Rollins, leading lady in *No Stronger Love*.

Yeah. Me. Auditioning. On a stage. In front of people. How did I get here, again? Oh, right. I made the mistake of telling my best friend, Ainsley, that I wanted to step outside of my comfort zone. I was thinking something along the lines of trying a caramel latte instead of a vanilla one, but my BFF convinced me to try out for the most recent production at the community theater.

I can't decide if it's better or worse that I work here—behind the scenes, of course. So behind the scenes, I doubt most of the people here will recognize me. We're a small but respected theater, and I make up the entire accounting department. I don't mind. The less noticeable I am, the better.

So, walking onto this stage, literally standing in the spotlight, is unnerving on every level. I close my eyes and focus on breathing in through my nose, out through my mouth, like my therapist taught me. I feel as though my heart is about to break through my ribcage, it's pounding so hard. A thin sheen of cold sweat dots my brow and upper lip, and my hands shake as I reach for the script I have tucked away under my cardigan.

That's another thing. I'm dressed like a grandma in my starched white blouse, buttoned all the way up to the top. The other women here have on clothes more appropriate for a nightclub, which I suppose fits more with the character than my work attire. However, there's not much I can do about that now.

With a final cleansing breath, I square my shoulders, lift my head, and open my eyes.

I close them again. And then blink them open. There's no way I'm staring at Weston Cooper Haze, right? I try blinking him away again, but he's still there. *What the heck?*

Maybe it's just someone who looks like him. That makes sense. He's won all kinds of awards; I don't even know how many or what kind, just that his name is thrown around every time there's an award show. Of course there are people who emulate his style. But what about those unmistakable green eyes?

I'm not a huge fangirl or anything, but I mean, come on. The man is gorgeous. Black hair, green eyes, and a strong, sharp jaw that always has a five o'clock shadow. And let's not get started on those muscles I know he's hiding under his shirt. The man has been shirtless on the big screen multiple times, and yeah, I've taken my fill of his perfectly chiseled body.

"Shay?" Reggie's surprised tone breaks through my thoughts.

God, what is wrong with me? I just need to bumble my way through this audition, which is sure to be a disaster, then scamper back into my office tucked away on the second floor and hide under my desk. Yes, that's the plan. Then I can tell my best friend I did it, and maybe she'll let me stay in my comfort zone for another year or two.

"Yes," I squeak out. This is going great so far.

"Are you... are you lost? Do you need something?"

The man who can't possibly be Weston Cooper Haze glares at Reggie, almost as if he didn't like his tone and wants to say something about it. Weird. I clear my throat and try again. I promised Ainsley I'd give it my all. Even though she went and married a mountain man and now lives in Montana, a promise is a promise.

Besides, I need to rebuild my courage now more than ever since Ainsley has found her happily ever after. I can't drag her down with my fears and doubts anymore. It's up to me to take the first step in healing. This is the bravest thing I've done since... nope. Can't go there. I can't think about him.

"I'm here to audition," I say with more confidence than I feel. Reggie's eyebrows fly up to his hairline as his mouth drops open slightly. The movie star look-alike grins. Holy. Cow. He's *beautiful*. Those green eyes sparkle with warmth and a hint of mischief.

"For the play?" Reggie asks, apparently still confused. I get it. I'm pretty much a mouse around here. I wasn't always this way, but everything changed three years ago. Now I like keeping my head down and going unnoticed.

"Yes," I tell him, more firmly this time.

"Oh, right, yes. Well, then, let's get on with it," he stutters out, clearly flustered by my presence. He knows as well as I do that this is going to be a shitshow.

I roll my shoulders and take a deep breath, trying not to look at the Weston Cooper Haze doppelgänger but my eyes find his, despite my best efforts. Our gazes lock, and all the air drains out of my lungs. My ears start ringing, but I can't look away. He looks as confused and disoriented as I feel, and yet he can't tear his eyes away from me, either. The intensity of the moment bears down on me, making me feel light-headed.

And then the man winks at me. Dammit. My skin prickles with awareness, and a shiver works its way down my spine, landing right between my legs. Holy crap, are my panties wet? When's the last time that happened?

He nods his head, silently encouraging me to continue. Something about that settles me. This man seems to want me to audition, and suddenly I want whatever he wants.

With trembling hands, I look down at the script and reread the lines in the heroine's monologue. It's an intense scene, one where she declares her strength and demands the kind of love most people only dream about. I almost laugh at the thought of me portraying someone like that.

I close my eyes and let the words fall from my lips, wishing I could be as bold as Seneca.

"I'm no damsel in distress, and if I am, I'll be my own white knight. I refuse to become that girl again, the one who wilted and withered away, silently decaying behind closed doors." I pause to take a breath, but I don't dare open my eyes. "Do I want love? Yes, but on my own terms. I'm not a kept woman. Not anymore. I want a partner, a protector, a friend. I want a-a... a... l-lover." I stumble over the word, feeling self-conscious about saying it in front of the two men judging me right now. "But more than that, I want to be respected and seen for who I am. I want someone to challenge me as much as they cherish me. I want it all. And I won't settle for anything less. Are you that man? Will you give me everything?"

All I can hear is my pulse pounding in my ears. All I can feel is my heart rattling around in my chest. When I open my eyes, all I can see is the deep green gaze of the handsome movie star body double.

Reggie leans over and whispers something to him, but the man either doesn't hear or doesn't care. His eyes never leave mine. I can't quite place the look he has. It's like he's tearing me apart piece by piece, trying to dig down into the very core of who I am.

"Thanks for auditioning," Reggie says after clearing his throat. "I'm not sure if you're right for the part."

I nod my head, ignoring the sinking feeling in my stomach. I knew this was coming. Heck, I even wanted to be rejected. Why, then, do I feel disappointment and shame flood through every cell in my body?

"What?" the gorgeous man says, finally breaking eye contact with me. "Why would you say that?" He looks angry, a fact that Reggie picks up on right away.

"I... well, the lines. They weren't, uh, very believable," he chokes out while shuffling a stack of papers in front of him.

"But she wants to believe them," he says, turning his gaze on me once again. How the heck did he know that? "That's the best motivation for an actor. She's going to be brilliant. I already see her growing into the role."

I know my face is bright red. I must not have heard him correctly. He's fighting for me to get the part? Why? I don't even want it. I think. Is he in the play? Maybe it wouldn't be so bad working with a man who looks like a Hollywood movie star...

Both men are looking at me now, apparently waiting for a response. What was the question?

"Uh..."

"I'll prove it. Let's run the scene together." Without waiting for approval from Reggie, he runs up to me, jumping onto the stage in one graceful move.

His presence is overwhelming. This close to him, I can see the defined muscles rippling through his shirt. He smells like cedar and spice, with a hint of something else. Something unique and purely masculine. He's so close to me now I can feel the warmth radiating off his body. I have to tip my head all the way back to look him in the eyes. The man is tall, that's for sure. Tall, broad shouldered, intimidatingly handsome, and most definitely not a body double.

"Wow," I whisper under my breath. My cheeks heat up at my dorky, awkward introduction, but I can't seem to stop. "You're really him? Weston Cooper Haze?"

He gives me a lopsided grin that has me feeling all sorts of things. He looks boyish and playful. I don't know how I know this, but I get the sense he hasn't smiled like this in a long time.

"You can call me Weston," he says with a hint of amusement in his voice.

"Oh. Right. Weston. You're, um, you're in the play? This play?" I'm sure my face is beet red at this point. Who knew my first attempt at stepping outside my comfort zone would land me in the presence of Hollywood royalty? Yet, when I look at him, that's not what I see. He's more than his profession, just like I'm more than mine.

"I'll be starring opposite you," he says with all the confidence in the world. "Here, let's finish the scene. You're brilliant. Don't mind Reggie. He seems like a prick."

Reggie grunts and I try to muffle my giggle, but I can't. Reggie *is* kind of a prick, but no one would ever say that to his face. I suppose being famous has its perks. Weston smiles at me again, but it's softer this time. Almost tender.

I look down at the script, skimming ahead in the scene. My eyes pause and grow wide when I see the stage directions a few paragraphs down. I never got this far into the scene since I knew I was going to fail, but what I'm reading now has me breaking out in a cold sweat all over again. There's a kiss. One that's supposed to be "claiming and swoon-worthy".

"I, um, I don't know what I'm doing," I whisper, my eyes darting up to meet his before looking back down again. To my complete surprise, Weston reaches out and tips my chin up, his kind green eyes resting on mine.

"You're acting with me," he says with a grin. For some reason, that breaks the tension. I feel...safe. The feeling wraps its way around my body, securing me and anchoring me to him. It's been so damn long since I've been this comfortable around someone, or hell, comfortable in my own skin. How did he manage to do that?

I nod and nibble on my bottom lip, trying unsuccessfully to hide my smile. Clearing my throat, I read the last line of my monologue, this time with my eyes wide open and trained right on Weston's.

"Are you that man? Will you give me everything?"

"Everything. All of me. I'll be whatever you need. Protector, best friend, supporter. Lover," he says with an honest to God twinkle in his eye. His face suddenly grows serious as he reaches up to cup the side of my face. Holy wow, I can feel his touch everywhere. "I love you, Seneca. I love you."

My breath catches in my throat and tears sting the back of my eyes. I don't think anyone has ever said that to me before. My parents aren't exactly warm and fuzzy, and the nannies they hired to raise me were just there for the paycheck. I'm not sure if it counts in this scenario, but God, the way he's looking at me, I could almost swear he means it.

His green eyes are soft, yet intense and full of...*something*. Once again, I can't decipher the look he's giving me. Weston's thumb gently caresses my cheek as we continue to stare at each other. I have no idea what my line is, but I can't bring myself to break this connection.

"Well, when you're right, you're right!" Reggie declares, shattering the moment Weston and I were sharing. Weston looks irritated, which makes me smile for some reason. Was he feeling it, too? Does he know what his words mean to me, however fake they may be? Oh Lordy, I don't know if my heart can take working with this man.

"Of course, I'm right," Weston grunts, looking over at Reggie before meeting my gaze once more. His hand is still cupping my face like he wants to keep me right here with him. I don't think I could move if I wanted to. "What do you say? Will you be my leading lady?"

Panic and anxiety flood through me, ripping me away from the fantasy. "I..."

"It'll be fun," he says, sliding his hand down my arm and taking my hand in his. "I was dreading this, but now I can't wait to get started."

I'm not sure why he's here if he was dreading this, but his words make my stomach flutter... as well as other, lower parts of me. The man is seriously hot, seriously famous, and for some reason, very serious about wanting me in this role.

That's not the plan, though. I was going to do the audition and then hide in my office until I could go home and continue hiding under my blankets. I don't like being seen, but I want him to see me. I want him to know me. Almost as much as I want to know him. Maybe that's why I find myself nodding.

"Yeah, I'm all yours," I whisper. "I-I mean, your leading lady. Um, I mean I'll do it. The play. With you. Oh my God," I mutter, burying my face in my hands. I'm so awkward. This isn't a great start.

"Excellent!" Reggie exclaims. I'll send you the schedule for rehearsals this afternoon. I'm sure you can work around your regular hours here at the theater."

I drop my hands from my face and nod, trying to get myself together.

Weston takes my hand again, squeezing it gently. He leans down, close enough to brush his lips against the shell of my ear. "For the record," he whispers, "you were right the first time. You're all mine." He presses the sweetest kiss on my temple, making me gasp softly. I look up at him in shock, but Weston just winks at me. "See you for our first rehearsal, Shay."

With that, he jumps down from the stage, leaving me gaping after him. What the heck just happened? Am I really doing this?

Chapter 3

Weston

"You don't need to check up on me every damn day, Linda," I grumble into the phone as I gather my keys and wallet.

"I disagree. Someone needs to make sure you stay out of trouble and make it to your first day of rehearsal," she snips, making me scrub a hand down my face.

"I didn't like it when my mom nagged me and I like it even less when you do it," I mutter under my breath. I know it's all about business and protecting her paycheck, but Jesus, I'm thirty-three, not twelve. "Plus, I've been good all week, haven't I?"

"Fair enough," she sighs. "I'll limit my calls to once a week. I'm working on a few things from my end. I'll email you a list of approved charities for you to choose from. Donating will help your image..."

I tune out as she rambles on. I know I should probably pay attention, seeing as it's my career on the line, but my thoughts drift toward Shay, as they have nearly every waking moment since I last saw her a week ago.

Hell, I even dream about her. Those soft curves, her big doe eyes, and full, pouty lips that make her look like the most precious doll. I see her tentative smile when I close my eyes and hear her sweet, soft voice when I drift off to sleep. There's no doubt this woman already has a hold on me.

I hang up with Linda, making a note to check in with my agent to get a recap of whatever the hell she just told me. I slide into the sleek SUV I rented for the two months I'll be here in Seattle, adjusting the rear view mirror. I'm almost shocked to see the smile on my face. I didn't even realize I was doing it. I also didn't realize how good it felt. When's the last time I was this excited for a new project? And who would have guessed it would be for the play I was dreading just one week ago?

It's all because of Shay. I can't explain it and I find I don't want to. She's beauty personified, that's for damn sure, but it's so much more than that. I still feel the softness of her skin from where I held her face. Still smell her sweet honey and jasmine perfume. Or maybe it's her shampoo. Either way, it's intoxicating and I can't wait to get close enough to smell it again.

I grin at myself and shake my head as I pull into the parking lot of the little theater. Who would have thought I'd be jonesing to sniff a woman? I'm not mad about it, though. This is the lightest I've felt in so long. Maybe ever. I loathe Teresa with every fiber of my being, but some part of me will always be thankful that she inadvertently sent me straight into the arms of Shay. Well, not quite in her arms just yet, but soon.

When I get to the back entrance of the theater, I see the object of my obsession already standing by the door. She looks over one shoulder, then the other, before repeating the process. Her movements are jerky and she's tense, her shoulders hunched as she keeps her head down. It's as if she's expecting someone to jump out of the shadows.

A surge of protectiveness hits me square in the chest, the force of it pushing all the air out of my lungs. Someone made her afraid of her own shadow. That someone will answer to me soon enough.

I start moving toward her without realizing I'm doing it. My body moved on its own, understanding my need to be close to her before my brain could catch up. Shay snaps her head in my direction and jumps back, letting out a startled gasp. I curse myself for scaring her and swallow down another wave of anger at whoever put the fear in her eyes.

Holding my hands out to show her I'm no threat, I slowly step up next to her. Her eyes go soft with recognition and relief when she sees me. "Sorry, didn't mean to startle you, sunshine."

Shay's eyes widen ever so slightly at my endearment for her. I didn't mean for it to slip out, but I don't regret it. I've been calling her sunshine in my head all week. That's what she is. Bright and airy as sunlight, even through her anxiety and fear.

"Weston Cooper Haze," she says with a smile. God, her voice. It's soft and sweet like the rest of her, but with a slightly raspy edge that makes her undeniably sexy and sultry. She's effortlessly gorgeous and every single thing about her is irresistible. I can tell she's a little star struck, but something about her is so damn genuine I know she'd never give me false praise to cater to my ego. Fuck if that doesn't make me like her even more. "It's alright. Just nerves, I guess," she says, shrugging and looking away from me.

A few strands of the lightest blonde hair I've ever seen escapes from where she had them pinned back. My hand moves on its own, much like it did during her audition when I cupped her cheek. I reach out, taking her golden locks between my thumb and forefinger, and gently rub back and forth. It's silky smooth and somehow warms me through and through, like a ray of sunshine.

Shay blinks up at me, those big brown eyes full of questions and more than a little longing. I want to gather her up in my arms and promise her the world, but I don't want to scare her away. I tuck her hair behind her ear, resisting the urge to kiss her, though just barely.

"Ready?" I ask, taking a step back from her to open the door. Shay nods her head and takes a deep breath. She stands up a little straighter like she's bracing herself for battle. I get the sense she really is fighting a personal war, one that no one else sees. No one but me. I see her slaying her demons one by one as she steps into the theater.

My career is studded with award shows and pats on the back, but never have I felt the sense of satisfaction and pride as I do now, watching Shay work through her anxiety and rise to the challenge. The feeling is so overwhelming I'm almost light-headed. It's not lost on me that I relate to my role as a true romantic who found *the one* more and more each day. The thing is, I think I like it.

The spell is only broken when Shay looks at me over her shoulder, giving me one of those small, genuine smiles of hers. I'll cherish every one of them. "You coming?" she asks, her eyes twinkling with a playfulness I haven't seen before. I want to bring that out in her more often.

"Lead the way, sunshine."

She blushes at my name for her, which, yeah, has my cock hardening in my jeans. I have a feeling this might be a bit of a problem while on set. It's worth it to be next to her.

I can't help but follow her around like a shadow. I'm just that drawn to her. She knows some people, while others she's meeting for the first time. I notice her tensing up when a big dude walks up to her and holds out his hand for her to shake. I'm by her side in a second, ready to punch the fucker in the nose. Linda would murder me, but I don't care.

My hand finds the small of her back, gently letting her know I'm here. Shay relaxes ever so slightly, making me want to beat my chest like a caveman. She trusts me. Or, at the very least, her subconscious knows I'll always keep her safe.

"I'm Eric, one of the stagehands," the man says, first addressing Shay and then me.

"N-nice to meet you," she stutters out before clearing her throat. The tremble in her voice has me tucking her into my side. I can't help it. "I'm Shay," she says with more confidence. "I'm playing the part of Seneca."

After we make our introductions, Shay is whisked away by the assistant director to review her schedule. I'm about to follow her when Reggie calls for me to go over something. I roll my eyes and let out an exasperated breath, not looking forward to spending the day with Reggie.

Shay looks at me over her shoulder with a barely suppressed grin on her face, like she knows exactly what I'm thinking. "Good luck," she whispers.

"You, too, sunshine," I say with a wink. Damn, that blush. I wonder if it goes all the way down her chest, making her perky little breasts bright pink. I wonder if she'll let me see.

The rest of the day is spent working through some rough patches in the script. I haven't done a lot of theater, but I did a few performances early in my career and one a couple of years ago. I've always enjoyed it, but it doesn't pay even half as well as the big screen. Nothing does, really. Then again, nothing else requires your soul the way Hollywood does. Suddenly the idea of going back feels wrong. Especially going back without Shay.

I'm able to sneak away a few times to check in on my sunshine. She's still anxious, that's for sure, but she has these moments of absolute brilliance, where her defenses crumble and her nerves melt away. Whether it's laughing with a friend or delivering a line with confidence, Shay is absolutely stunning. But then her light dims and she shrinks back into herself like she didn't mean to be so bold.

Who made you hide your light?

I'll get to the bottom of that, but for now, I'll hang on to these little windows into her heart. She's so full of life; she just needs someone to remind her it's worth living again. I don't know how I know that, only that I feel the truth of it in every cell of my being. I'm going to be that person. Starting today.

Reggie announces the end of rehearsal and reminds us what scenes we're running tomorrow and who needs to show up. I don't waste a second finding Shay again. It's been too damn long since her eyes were on mine. Never have I had this desire to be in someone's presence. No, not desire. Need.

"How was the first day?" I ask once I'm standing right next to her. She jumps a little bit and I curse myself for startling her again. I'll have to be better about that. Subtlety and caution have never been my style, but I find I'd do just about anything to make this woman comfortable around me.

"Good," she lies. Her brown eyes dart up to mine, a hint of guilt swimming in her deep brown irises. "Overwhelming," she admits, looking down at her feet.

I tilt her chin up, forcing her to meet my gaze. "For me, too."

"Really? I mean, you do this all the time with much higher stakes and bigger budgets."

I shrug. "Sure, but there are always those first day jitters. I usually have to do a few breathing exercises before stepping onto the set for the first time."

I'm not sure why I told her that. It's true, the start of every new project feels overwhelming, but that's not something I share with people. It's easier to shove those feelings down and go with the flow, fake it till you make it and whatnot. But what do you do when you've made it and now you're just... fake?

Looking down at Shay, I don't regret opening up even just that little bit. If it helped ease some of her anxiety, I'm happy to tell her anything and everything she wants to know about me. Yet another feeling this woman has brought out in me.

"I do that, too!" she says with a pure, genuine smile. She's so beautiful it makes my chest ache. Other, lower parts of me are also aching. I've been hurting for her all day, my stubborn dick refusing to give up the fight. "Not that I go on many sets, but just, like, in general. Life's kind of overwhelming, you know?" I can tell it took a lot of courage for her to say that.

"Want to talk about it over coffee?" I blurt out. I cringe at my very obvious, very awkward way of asking her out. I've never had trouble talking to women—in fact, I'm usually trying to brush them off, but Shay has me all twisted up. I want to taste her lips, her skin, the sweetness between her thighs. God, I want to sink my thickness deep inside of her and make her come so many times she passes out.

But more than that, I want to comfort her. I want to be her safe place. I want to wake up next to her in the middle of the night and pull her close, just so I can hold her in my sleep. These tender, protective, possessive feelings are all new to me, but I'm not scared of them. They've given me a purpose. I haven't had one in so long.

"Oh... um..." Shay furrows her brow and worries her bottom lip. I swear I can see every thought in her head as they flash across her face. Confusion, surprise, and a spark of excitement. I wait for her to say yes, but then she curls back into herself. I can see the light draining from her eyes, the golden flecks dimming and then sputtering out. "I can't. Um, thanks, though."

Damn. I've been rejected for movie roles, awards, and most recently from my own career until I pay my dues, but nothing stings like hearing those words fall from her lips. I'm not giving up, however. No way am I letting this incredible woman slip through my fingers.

I remind myself to slow the hell down as I plaster a smile on my face. Shay looks like she's bracing herself for me to say something awful to her. I realize I put her in an awkward situation. I kick myself for what feels like the hundredth time today. I need to get my head in the game if I want a chance with Shay.

Good thing I know where to find her every single day for the next two months. I think I can win my woman over in that time.

"No worries, sunshine," I say with a grin, hoping to put her at ease. "It gets better from here," I tell her, stepping back a bit even though it pains me. I don't want to crowd her. "Every day gets a little easier. Who knows, you might even love acting."

"I'm not so sure about that," she mumbles. It's not the first time I've wondered what made her want to audition, but I'm certainly not complaining.

"Give it a chance. It's awkward at first, but then there's a moment when it clicks. You connect with the character and find yourself thinking about what they would think, instead of what you think they'd think." I pause and laugh at my confusing sentence. "That made a lot more sense in my head."

"No, I get it. It's like the role takes on a life of its own. It's no longer a series of directions and dialogue, but something you want to experience and live up to."

"Exactly," I say with a grin. "You'll be a movie star yet."

I haven't thought about why I like acting, or even if I like acting at all in... well, I don't know if I've ever thought about it. It was a paycheck. A nice one. One that got me out of the trailer park I grew up in and into a ten-bedroom villa with an infinity pool overlooking Malibu beach.

Our eyes lock and we share another moment like we did at her audition. I can't look away. Her intense, brown eyes hold so much uncertainty, but those golden flecks are back, shining with more than a little curiosity. I can work with that.

I tuck another loose strand of hair behind her ear, entirely too happy when she doesn't pull away from me. "You have beautiful hair," I murmur.

"Really?" Shay smooths her hands over her icy blonde hair self-consciously.

"Absolutely gorgeous. It reminds me of sunshine," I say with a grin.

"I suppose sunshine isn't so bad," she whispers.

"Not so bad at all," I agree. As much as I don't want to say goodbye, I know I've pushed my luck for one day. "I'll see you tomorrow, yeah?"

"Yup," she confirms, nodding her head. "See you tomorrow, Weston."

She waves and heads to the back of the theater, where I assume her office is. Fuck, hearing my name on her lips isn't helping my dick calm down. I want to hear her whimper my name, I want her to scream it over and over until it's the only word she knows.

Soon, sunshine. Soon you'll know how much I want you.

Chapter 4

Shay

"So, is he that shredded in real life or is that all Photoshopped or whatever," Ainsley, the person responsible for this craziness, asks.

"It's not like he takes his shirt off during rehearsal," I laugh, throwing a piece of popcorn at her.

My bestie and her new husband, Brewer, are in the Seattle area for a couple of days so Brewer can drop off a few of his handmade furniture pieces at a local boutique. Her visit couldn't have come at a better time. When she waltzed into my apartment three hours ago, she insisted that we have a movie marathon starring none other than Weston Cooper Haze.

"Shame," she tuts, making me giggle. "I bet it's all real. I mean, just look at the man! He's ripped. Tell me he's that gorgeous up close."

I feel my cheeks heat up just thinking about what it felt like to be close to him. He's so much more than handsome, or *gorgeous*, as Ainsley likes to say. His green eyes aren't just mesmerizing, they're warm, curious, and a bit mischievous. I saw all of that in his gaze each time he snuck a glance at me during that first rehearsal last week. His smile isn't just breathtaking, it's genuine, at least when aimed at me. It's different than the one I see on the big screen, or doing interviews, or even when he's accepting awards.

"He smells like cedar and cinnamon," I blurt out. Why my brain chose that detail to share, I'm not sure. God, this man has me all out of sorts. I think I like it, though. I know it's nothing more than a crush—one that I share with millions of people across the world, but still. Feeling safe enough around someone to entertain fantasies of a relationship is healing, in a way. "And he sort of asked me out." Well, damn. I didn't mean to let that slip, either.

"Shay!" Ainsley screeches. "Why am I just hearing about this? Tell me everything! When is the date? Where are you going? Oh! What are you wearing? No more button ups and cardigans for you. Let's go shopping! You're lucky I came back in time for this." She jumps off the couch as if we're going to go to the mall right now, at nine p.m.

"There's no date."

"What? Why not?" Ainsley is standing in front of me now, towering over me while I remain seated on the couch. Her hands are on her hips and she's giving me a hard look.

"Why not? First of all, he's a freaking movie star. I'm nowhere near his type. Second of all, he's trouble. Haven't you seen the articles about his crazy parties and getting arrested for assaulting a Russian or something? That's the last thing I should be looking for in a relationship."

"I won't even address the whole *not his type* thing, because it's BS and you know it deep down. As for the second, when have you ever known tabloids to tell the truth, the whole truth, and nothing but the truth?"

I glare at her, not liking that she's making some good points. "Well, even so. He's leaving when the play is over, so what's the point?"

"I'm not saying you should marry the guy, but what could one date hurt? I think it'd be really good for you."

"But he's a movie star," I say again, hoping she'll understand. "Everything he does is so... public. I don't want my picture plastered everywhere online."

Ainsley's face goes soft and she drops her hands from her hips, sitting down next to me on the couch. "Hun, Sean is gone. He's still in prison." I look down at my hands, trying not to let her see I'm on the verge of tears. "Your life has been on pause for three years now. It's time you start living again."

"I'm already doing the play," I whisper, not trusting my voice. "Isn't that enough?"

"Is it?" I lift my head to look at her, furrowing my brow. Ainsley sighs and takes my hand in hers. "Tell me, did Weston give off creepy stalker vibes?"

"No," I say without hesitating. I never felt uncomfortable around him. Quite the opposite, in fact. The way he followed me around during our first rehearsal wasn't in a predatory way. He was being protective. He let me lead the way and introduce myself, but when he sensed I was uncomfortable, he was right by my side.

"Did he seem aggressive or confrontational?"

I shake my head no, thinking about how things could have been awkward after I turned him down, but instead he smiled and moved on, making sure I knew it wasn't a big deal. "No, nothing like that. He was... sweet."

"Sweet?" Ainsley snorts. "The man who flipped off the paparazzi and punched a dude?"

"You're not exactly helping your case," I mutter.

"I meant it as a good thing. He's sweet to you. It's cute." I try to hide my smile and blush, but I know she sees it anyway. "Oh my God, you do like him! This is perfect. Think about how thrilled your parents would be to have Weston Cooper Haze as a son-in-law!"

We both erupt in laughter. "Yeah, at least that would save me from my mom trying to set me up with another one of their friend's sons." I meant it as a joke, but a shiver runs down my spine remembering how disastrous the set up with Sean went.

Ainsley continues with the joke—I'm sure she's trying to break me out of my sudden turn of thoughts. "Wasn't the last one like, fifty?"

"Forty-eight," I say with a grimace, trying to ground myself in the moment instead of letting fear sweep me away. "And he was no silver fox, I'll tell you that much."

"Ew. You know I understand how awful that life is. But all the more reason to be proactive about this! Take control of your life again, Shay.

I promise you won't regret it." She gives my hand a final squeeze before settling back in for the rest of our movie marathon.

***

"Shay, sweetie, I'm so glad you called. What are you doing on Friday night?"

"I have rehearsal, Mom," I tell her for the fifth time.

"You're still in that silly play? Honestly, I don't know what you're trying to prove."

"It's only been a week. And I wanted to try something different," I mumble, hating how her harsh tone still cuts me deep. I'm twenty-one, but when she talks to me like this I feel like I'm a little kid being scolded for speaking out of turn.

"If you want different, you should move back home to Bainbridge Island. I don't like you being all the way out there in the city. You're never going to find a decent man in a place like that."

"I can't commute for an hour and a half on the ferry every day for my job," I point out.

"You'll quit, of course. Honestly, it's time you stop hiding out in that old theater, anyway. That little incident was years ago. We'll find you a good husband from a good family and you'll forget all about it. That's why you should drop out of the play and come to dinner Saturday evening. Paul and Leslie and their son, Victor, will be here."

I pull the phone away from my face so I can sigh without her hearing me. I knew I shouldn't have called my mother, but I feel safer talking to someone on the phone when I'm walking alone.

"I'm not quitting the play or my job, I'm not moving home, and I'm not looking for a relationship right now," I tell her. It's not the first time we've had this conversation and it won't be the last. It's taken me a lot of therapy to figure out how to set boundaries with my parents and it's still difficult in the best of times. Thinking about having dinner with a man who isn't Weston, however, instills a surprising amount of strength behind my words. I'm not sure why, since we're not together or anything, but I'll take whatever modicum of confidence I can get.

I'm over being hurt by the fact that neither she nor my father even believed me about Sean at first. They were both in Paris at the time of the *incident* and they didn't come home, saying I was being overdramatic. It wasn't until they visited me in the hospital that the truth finally sank in.

Did they stop trying to make me a trophy wife? Of course not. As soon as the bruises faded, they were back on their game.

My mom insists that marriage will help me "get over it", and she's made it her life mission to marry me off to the richest bachelor who can secure future business deals and contribute to the family wealth.

"Well, you don't have to get snippy with me," she says defensively. "I just wish you would at least consider coming back home."

"Look, I've got to go, Mom. I'm almost at the thea—umph!" I run right into someone, cutting off the rest of my sentence. "Oh!" I gasp, stumbling backward. Large, comforting, warm hands grasp my upper arms, keeping me steady. The familiar cedar and spice scent wraps around me, making my heart stutter and my stomach flip.

"You alright, sunshine?"

God, his voice. How can a voice turn me on so much? I've never noticed it before when watching his movies, but hearing it in real life, when he's standing so close with his hands still on me... whew, let's just say my cheeks are on fire and I feel a pressure building in my lower belly.

"Who is that?!" my mother shrieks, her voice breaking me of my lustful thoughts. "Shay? Who is talking to you?"

"I, uh, I have to call you back, Mom," I whisper.

"Shay, don't you hang up on—"

Too late. I hang up and shove my phone in my pocket, taking a step away from Weston. A coldness sweeps through me when he drops his hands from my arms. "Sorry," I murmur. I try looking away from him, but I can't. Something about his green eyes pulls me in, pulls me under, and drowns me in his intensity.

"It's no problem," he says with an easy smile. "Are you alright?" he asks again.

"Oh. Yeah, yeah, I'm good. Just my mom driving me nuts." I roll my eyes and grin at him, loving when he grins back.

Weston cups the back of my neck, gently drawing me closer to him. My body relaxes at his touch, even as my breathing grows shallow and my heart picks up speed. He bends down, brushing his lips against the shell of my ear, much like he did the day of my audition.

"Love seeing that smile, Shay. You're breathtaking." He places the lightest kiss right below my ear, making me shiver.

He thinks I'm beautiful? Is this for real or are we acting?

"Th-thanks. Um, you, too." Oh my God, could I be any more of a spaz? I'm sure my face is beet red. Weston chuckles and takes a step back, giving me some much needed space.

"Glad you think so, baby. Does that mean you're ready for our scene today?"

I didn't think I could blush any harder, but thinking about what we're rehearsing today practically has my entire body flushing. It's the first kiss. I know it's childish to get so worked up over something like that. Especially since it's a play and none of it's real. But I've only been kissed twice, though I'm not sure either of them count. Charlie in seventh grade kissed me on a dare, and my prom date made a move before I was ready and I just froze until the sloppy kiss was over.

I haven't done anything else with anyone. Ever. Add in what happened with Sean, and I was pretty sure I'd never want to try again.

"Not at all," I tell him truthfully. He gives me that impossibly sexy smirk of his.

"That's the best place to start."

For some reason, his reply makes me laugh. It feels good. *Really* good. Like breathing for the first time after being trapped underwater.

Weston opens the door for me and guides me inside with his hand on my lower back. We've only been rehearsing for a few days, but he's found little ways to touch me, both on and off the set. I won't lie, I kind of love it. I don't like being the center of attention, but I think I like the attention Weston gives me. He's just as protective and kind as he was before he asked me out, and he hasn't pressured me or made me feel awkward at all. The thing is, I think I'd like him to try again. I might break and tell him yes.

The first thirty minutes of rehearsal are dedicated to announcements, updates, and other housekeeping items for the cast and crew. Reggie wraps it up, reminding us where we need to be for the day. Hopefully nothing important was said because I didn't hear a single word.

I was too focused on how I'll be kissing Weston freaking Cooper freaking Haze shortly. Holy crap. I really didn't think this one through, did I? I knew there was kissing, but I chose to ignore those parts. It didn't seem real until he reminded me what scene we're doing today.

"Hey," Weston says, resting his hand on my shoulder. Once again, I feel like I can breathe now that he's near. "I can talk to Reggie if you're not feeling up for running this scene today. I'm sure there's other stuff we can work on."

This man. He's so sweet. At least to me. I get a tiny confidence boost, remembering what Ainsley said. For some reason, I bring out a side of him no one else gets to see. It makes me trust him and hope that he can bring out a side of me that's been all but forgotten.

"No, I'm ready," I tell him truthfully.

"Me too," he says, giving me an adorable lopsided grin. Weston offers me his hand, helping me out of my seat. "See you out there." He nods toward the stage and gives my hand a squeeze before heading backstage. I need a few moments to collect myself, so I dash to the bathroom before we officially start.

By the time I return, everyone is getting in position. I'm not on stage at the beginning of the scene, so I hang off to the side, watching Weston get into character and deliver his lines. He truly is talented. I've watched a lot of plays here at the theater, and subsequently, I've seen my fair share of actors with varying talents.

No one commands the room quite like Weston. Sure, he's had a long acting career and more experience than most of the part-timers who do these plays on the side, but it's more than that. There's a strength that runs deeper than confidence. I get the feeling Weston would be this way no matter what profession he ended up in.

"That's your cue," one of the stagehands whispers.

"Right, thanks," I say with a small smile, feeling dumb for messing up already. I scurry out on stage, my nerves threatening to choke me, but then slow down when my eyes lock on Weston's. I swear he's infusing some of his strength right into the marrow of my bones with the way he's looking at me.

His kind, patient eyes calm me down, reminding me to breathe and stand up tall. I'm Seneca Rollins and I'm about to put this man in his place.

"And just what do you think you're doing here, Mr. Calson?" I say with renewed inspiration.

Weston flashes me a brilliant smile, and is that a hint of pride I see? Why does that make me feel ten feet tall and invincible? He snaps back into character, but I'll hang on to that look and the feeling it brought me for the rest of my life; I already know it.

"I'm here to take you out to dinner," he says, taking a step closer to where I'm standing with my hands on my hips.

"I'm not hungry."

"Coffee, then." Weston takes another step toward me.

"Never touched the stuff," I respond, my voice less convincing this time as I take two steps in his direction.

"Drinks?" He's smiling now, closing the distance between us in three strides.

I shake my head no, tipping my head back to look up at him. Can he hear my heart rattling around in my ribcage? I feel his breath on my skin, the sensation sending a shiver down my spine.

"How about this, then?" Weston asks, bending down so his lips are a few inches from mine. I suck in a breath, every nerve ending in my body firing off at once. My stomach churns, but I'm not sure if it's because I'm about to have a panic attack, or because I'm so turned on my body can't even handle it. "Look at me," he whispers. It's so soft, I know his words are meant just for me. His hand comes up to cup the side of my face, his thumb rubbing my cheek back and forth in a soothing motion. "It's just us. Forget everyone and everything else. Be here with me, sunshine. Right here with me."

"I'm here with you," I whisper back.

Weston gives me one last look to make sure I'm okay, and then his lips touch mine, briefly at first, and then more firmly. The racing thoughts and overwhelming doubts come to a screeching halt and then scatter until there's nothing left but this kiss.

I sink into his embrace, letting him wrap his arm around my waist and pull me against him. His lips part beneath mine, the very tip of his tongue snaking out to lick my bottom lip before he breaks our kiss.

I don't know what comes over me, but I'm not done with him yet. My hands move almost without my permission, sliding up his chest and fisting his shirt, drawing him back to me. His eyes go dark, making me gasp softly before his mouth is on mine, claiming me with more intensity this time.

Weston breathes me in as he consumes me, coaxing me to open my lips and let him in. As soon as I do, a sharp whistling sound shatters the moment, breaking the connection we just shared. Weston grunts, turning his head toward Reggie while keeping his arm around me, holding me close.

Crap. I forgot about everyone else, just like Weston told me to. I know we were supposed to kiss, and that everyone else expected the kiss, but it still feels like we did something wrong. Maybe it's because it didn't feel fake. It felt like the most real thing I've ever experienced.

"Boy, you two have chemistry, that's for damn sure," Reggie says. "Who knew you had it in you, Shay?"

Weston glares at him, clenching his jaw while I look away, unable to face Reggie right now. "We're taking five," Weston growls before tugging me backstage. I gladly follow. I need the safety of the shadows right now.

As soon as we're behind the curtain, Weston leads me to a secluded hallway. He spins me around, sliding his hands down to my hips as he presses me against the wall. Weston rests his forehead on mine, taking a deep breath. I can feel his hands tremble from where he's holding me. Am I doing that to him?

"Need to try that again," he growls softly, his voice rough and needy. It sends liquid heat coursing throughout my body, landing a devastating blow to my throbbing sex.

I whimper something unintelligible, my own lust rendering me speechless. His eyes turn almost black as he closes the distance between us once more.

This kiss is different. Wilder. Rougher. A low, gravelly sound rumbles up through his chest as he pins me against the wall. His lips part and he licks inside my mouth, tangling our tongues together. I moan into his mouth as he deepens the kiss, wrapping his arms around my waist as I curl my arms around his neck.

He swallows down my desperate cry, muffling the sound and pulling my body closer against his. I can feel the tight muscles he has packed into his chest and stomach. Coupled with the way his strong arms are holding me tightly, and the obvious erection digging into my stomach, I nearly whimper again as I melt into his embrace.

He tears his mouth from mine, only to continue undoing me with light, teasing kisses down my neck. "Weston," I whisper, barely getting the word out before his lips find mine once more.

My body moves on its own, grinding against his, seeking some relief for the ache he's created deep inside. He groans, the sound almost painful as he pushes me against the wall and presses his body against mine. I feel his hands roam up and down my curves, leaving a trail of goosebumps as they go.

He grips my hips, squeezing them and then gently pushing me away as he backs up. "Gotta stop now, sunshine. Before we go too far."

I nod my head, pulling air into my lungs. "Right," I manage to breathe out. I'm not sure what he's talking about, or why he even brought me back here to kiss me in the first place. Was I so bad he wanted to give me lessons or something? I try not to let the confusion and hurt show, but apparently, I still have a long way to go in the acting department.

"Hey. Nothing like that, sweetheart. I want you," he murmurs, pulling me against him once again so I can feel exactly how much he wants me. "So much that I forgot where we were. This isn't the place, but trust me, Shay. Trust me that this isn't over."

He gives me one last chaste kiss on the lips, then steps back and adjusts himself. Wow, I mean, he felt pretty damn big when I was shamelessly rubbing against him, but that bulge is even more impressive than I thought.

"Don't look at me like that," he groans, making me giggle. "Love that laugh of yours, though. You can do that any time."

"Even when I'm staring at your, uh... your..." I feel myself blush, but I don't look away from him. It's been forever since I've flirted with someone, but Weston makes me feel bold. Well, bold for me.

My knees nearly give out when he gives me a wicked smirk. "While it's not normally the reaction I'd like, I don't mind. As long as you're happy." He darts his eyes away from me, rubbing the back of his neck and clearing his throat. Oh my gosh, is he blushing? Is he embarrassed to admit that?

"I'm happy," I tell him, gaining even more confidence as I take his hand in mine. "We better get back out there before Reggie comes looking for us."

"Lead the way, sunshine," he says with a chuckle.

Dragging Weston Cooper Haze on stage after he gave me the single hottest kiss in the history of kisses has me feeling like the queen of the world. I've never felt this powerful before.

Weston squeezes my hand, almost like he knew what I was thinking. I look at him over my shoulder and see the same look of pride in his sharp green eyes. It excites me and soothes me and has me feeling all sorts of other things I don't have time to analyze right now. I don't have to, though. One last look at him lets me know he feels it, too. Whatever this is, we're in it together.

Chapter 5

Weston

Her kiss absolutely wrecked me. I've been thinking about it for two damn weeks. I hate that our first kiss was in front of Reggie, of all people, but in the moment, it truly was just us. Just Shay and her soft, sweet lips. Shay and her honeyed, floral scent. Shay and her curvy body in my arms, against my chest, filling me up with her goodness and light.

I almost forgot we were on stage until Reggie so rudely interrupted our perfect connection. I wasn't nearly done with Shay, however. Part of me knew it wasn't the wisest move to take her to a dark hallway and devour her, but she was right there with me.

God, the way she molded her body to mine and clung to me while I kissed her the way we both needed... fuck. I'd be lying if I said I haven't jacked off to thoughts of her every damn day since. The fantasy doesn't end when I get off, though. Each time I come with her name on my lips, I picture us wrapped up in each other's arms after. I see her smile and the spark of life in her eyes, just like the day we kissed. It made me so damn proud of her.

I still don't know what made her hide herself away, but knowing I had something to do with bringing her out of her shell a little more had me smiling all day. Hell, I haven't been able to keep a smile off my face since. Even Linda noticed my change in attitude. She asked if I was on drugs, to which I laughed and assured her I wasn't. I'm not sure she believes me, but she hasn't stormed up here to check on me yet.

Shay and I have kissed a few times while rehearsing, though nothing like that first day. I didn't want to scare her off or make her think I only want her body. Make no mistake—I very much want to own every inch of her, but I want so much more. I want everything. That's what she is to me, and that's what I'll give her.

I still find ways to be alone with my sunshine, even when we're not scheduled to rehearse on the same day. The fact that she works at the theater has made my job easier, but I'd travel across the city for her if I had to. I'd travel across the whole damn country.

Every morning I meet her at the back door with coffee—she favored vanilla lattes the first week, but she switched to caramel lattes two days ago. When I asked why, she gave me an enigmatic smile and said she was trying something new. Something about the golden flecks glowing in her eyes made me think she's ready for a few more new things. Like letting me finally take her on that date.

"Morning!" Shay greets me, the excitement in her voice warming me up better than any coffee could.

"Hey, sunshine. Caramel latte for the leading lady," I say with a smile as I hand her the drink.

"You're spoiling me. Plus, all that sugar and whole milk is not doing my hips any favors."

I wrap my arm around her waist and pull her close, brushing my nose against hers. "You're perfect, and I plan on spoiling you a whole lot more, so you better get used to it."

I feel her breath on my lips and taste her sweetness on my tongue. She looks up at me with those big brown eyes, searing me with her questions and doubts. Beneath all of that, however, there's overwhelming hope and a longing so great it nearly brings me to my knees. She wants this as much as I do. She's ready to let me in, just a little, but she needs me to make the first move. I have no problem with that.

"Go out with me," I whisper, searching her eyes for any signs of distress.

"Is that a question or a demand," she sasses, a small smile curving up one side of her lips. I can't help but lean down and press a kiss there.

"It's whatever will get you to agree."

Shay nibbles on her bottom lip, a flash of uncertainty crossing her features. I see the moment she shuts down her fear and takes the leap, knowing I'll be right here to catch her. Shay nods her head and gives me the biggest, most beautiful smile I've ever seen.

"Need to hear you say it, sunshine."

"Yes," she murmurs, leaning a little closer to me.

"Yes, what?" I ask, dipping my head down to kiss the side of her neck. Her pulse throbs against my lips, making me groan softly while I kiss her there again.

"Y-yes I'll go out with you," she stutters out in a breathy voice.

"Finally," I grunt, kissing my woman for real. She immediately opens up for me, letting my tongue slide into her mouth so I can finally get another hit of my favorite drug.

Shay sighs so sweetly, melting into my embrace. I hold her closer, wanting to feel every inch of her. I hate the layers of clothing separating us. I want to touch her everywhere, feel her silky smooth skin, run my fingers over the curve of her hips, and the dip in her waist. Then I want to follow the same path with my tongue, feasting on her until she comes apart.

Unfortunately, Reggie chooses that moment to burst through the back door, making us both spring apart. It's not against the rules to date fellow cast members—I made sure to check, for Shay's sake, not mine. But I don't want to cause problems for Shay, especially when this is all so new.

"There you two are. Come on inside. We've only got a month left until opening night, but about three months' worth of work to get done," he says, his voice laced with annoyance. He's being overdramatic, as is expected with theater directors.

Shay clutches her caramel latte and ducks her head, following Reggie inside. I grab her hand, squeezing it, and smiling at her when she looks over her shoulder. I give her a wink and let her go, satisfied with the knowledge she'll be all mine tonight for our date.

***

My hands are shaking as I white knuckle the steering wheel on my way over to Shay's. I take a deep breath and try to relax. I've been on plenty of dates before, though most of them were for show. I've faced down crowds, critics, and paparazzi, but nothing has made me more nervous than the idea of messing this whole night up. One wrong move and I know I'll send Shay running. Not that I'd give up on her, but I know it would take time to build up her trust in me again.

I arrive at her apartment fifteen minutes early, so I decide to wait in my car for a bit. I don't want her to feel rushed, so I waste time triple checking my reservation at Purple, an upscale wine bar and restaurant in the heart of downtown Seattle.

The plan is to show her that I can do romance offscreen and offstage. Granted, I've never done anything like that before—which is part of the reason Teresa and I didn't work out. I can admit I was a shitty boyfriend, but she was no better. The more time I spend around Shay, the more I see how fucked up my last relationship was. We never cared about each other, so it didn't hurt when she cheated on me. It didn't hurt when we got in fights. It didn't hurt when we broke up. In fact, it felt like a relief.

The thought of losing Shay, on the other hand…

I growl and clench my fists up tight. We're not even "official" yet, but I already know this woman has woven her sunshine into the very fabric of my being. If she left me, I would unravel completely. Just one more reason I can't fuck this up.

The clock on the dashboard reads six fifty, ten minutes before I said I'd be here. Close enough. I can't wait another second to see her.

I have my nerves mostly under control, at least visibly, by the time I'm knocking at her door. There's silence for a few moments, making me panic. Did I get the address wrong? Is she standing me up? Did she—

"Just a minute!" her melodic voice rings out. I feel like I can breathe again as the tense muscles in my shoulders relax.

The door swings open to reveal my gorgeous sunshine in a light blue, A-line dress that hugs her chest and highlights her slim waist. It flares out at the hips and ends just above her knees. She's classy and beautiful and so fucking *mine* it hurts. Shay has on kitten heels that I somehow know haven't seen the light of day in a long time. Damn if I don't get that same overwhelming sense of pride knowing she brought them out of retirement for our date.

"Baby, you're stunning," I breathe out, my voice apparently stuck somewhere in my throat.

"Thanks."

I look up to meet her gaze, but her head is turned, looking at something inside her apartment. I follow her line of sight and see a conservative cardigan on a side table near the door. It only takes a second to realize what she's thinking. My girl is trying to decide if she wants to cover up. I hate that she feels the need to hide, but I'll do whatever it takes to make her feel comfortable.

"Want to grab a jacket or something? It might get chilly," I offer, giving her an excuse. She nods her head rapidly and grabs the cardigan. I reach out and take it out of her hands, opening it up to help her put it on.

Shay looks at me over her shoulder with an amused little grin on her face. If Matthew, Ted, and Linda could see me now, I doubt they'd even recognize me. I love it. I don't ever want to be the money hungry, aimless prick from before. That man didn't deserve someone as pure and precious as Shay. I'm still not worthy of her, but I'll spend the rest of my life trying to be everything she needs. Yeah, I'm already so far gone for this woman I'm planning forever. I just need her to get there, too.

"Thanks," she whispers as she turns around. I cradle her face in my hands and place a kiss on her forehead. When I pull away, Shay follows me and captures my lips with hers. Her move is bold and surprising and so damn sexy, I wrap my arms around her waist and haul her into my chest as I take everything she's offering me.

"I was trying to be a gentleman," I murmur into her parted lips before kissing her again. I can't help it. She's here in my arms, looking up at me with lust and longing in her eyes.

We're both panting for air by the time we break apart. "And here I was, trying to get the Hollywood heartthrob to kiss me," she sasses. A cute little blush stains her cheeks, but she never takes her eyes off me. I love seeing more of her personality. I love even more that I can bring it out in her.

"I don't know about the heartthrob business, but you can kiss me anytime, sunshine." She grins and goes back in for another kiss, but then her stomach rumbles loudly. I chuckle and give her one last chaste kiss. "Hold that thought. I promise we'll come back to it later."

Shay laughs softly, biting her bottom lip. How is she adorable and insanely sexy at the same time? I want to sink into her little pussy and feel her orgasm from the inside out, over and over, until we're both spent. Then I want to wrap her up in a blanket and cuddle her all night long. Yeah, that sounds pretty perfect to me.

We eventually make it out to my car after a few more lingering kisses, and I head toward the restaurant. I told her where we're going, and she seemed excited, but the closer we get to downtown, the more I feel Shay pull away from me. She's crawling back into her shell, and I'm not sure what I did or how to get us back to where we were only a few minutes ago.

"Everything okay?" I ask, taking her hand in mine. She squeezes it tightly, and I notice her hands are clammy and trembling slightly. "Sunshine? What's wrong?"

"Nothing," she's quick to say. Shay turns her head from where she was looking out the window, her big brown eyes finding mine. Just like every time she brushes off my concern, my girl looks guilty and then tells me the truth. I like that she can't seem to lie to me. "Are there going to be a lot of people there?"

"Probably." I know my answer was wrong when she tenses up and tries pulling her hand away. I rub my thumb over her knuckles, hoping to soothe her anxiety a bit. "But I got us a private table in the corner," I'm quick to say. "Just you and me." Shay nods her head but doesn't say anything for a few moments. "What are you thinking about, baby?" The silence is killing me.

"I just... are the paparazzi going to be there?"

I consider her question for a minute. Being photographed doing literally nothing has become the norm for me, but I know most people aren't used to the invasive press coverage. Shay doesn't just look like she's not used to it, though. She looks like she's on the verge of a panic attack. *Shit.*

"I really don't think so. No one knows I'm here in Seattle," I try to reassure her. She nods again, her eyes wandering toward the window as we get closer to the restaurant.

"Do you think... will other people take photos? Like on their phones? You're famous, after all."

Double shit. I should have planned something more low key. I wanted to impress her, but all I've done is made her anxious. Instead of turning right toward the restaurant, I hang a left and make my way to the place I'm renting.

"Change of plans," I announce when she gives me a questioning look. "I want to cook for you."

Her eyebrows just about disappear into her hairline. I'll take shocked over anxious any day. "You don't have to do that," she rushes to say. "Purple is great. It's a really nice restaurant. I haven't been there in years, but you should get to experience it while you're here."

There's a lot to unpack in that sentence. I wonder why it's been years since she's eaten at Purple. But more importantly, I hate that she still thinks I'm leaving when the play ends. Truthfully, I'm not sure what the plan is. The only thing I know is that being in a different state than Shay is unacceptable.

"We'll have time to go later," I promise her. "But I'd really like to have you in my space, if that's okay." She glances at me, letting me know she realizes what I'm doing. The grateful smile that tips up one corner of her lips confirms it was the right move.

Fifteen minutes later, we're pulling into the underground parking garage. I help Shay out of the car, ushering her inside the private elevator, straight to the penthouse. What can I say? I wanted to live in style when I came out here. Now I'm worried it'll be too much for her. That thought has literally never crossed my mind. What if she doesn't want all the lavish things and perks that come along with my fame and profession? Furthermore, what else do I really have to offer her?

Before I can spiral too much, the doors open to reveal the spacious living room and open kitchen. I watch Shay step inside and take it all in. She runs her delicate fingers over the back of the leather sectional, much the same way I want to run my fingers down the slope of her neck, the curve of her hip, up her inner thighs...

"Oh, wow! Look at that kitchen!" Shay's excited little outburst pulls me back from my lustful thoughts. "You can cook for me any time in here," she says dreamily as she makes her way to the top-of-the-line, newly remodeled kitchen.

Crap. In my mad dash to come up with a plan B for the evening, I forgot that I can't cook. Before I get the chance to tell her that, Shay spins around and beams at me. Goddamn, that golden spark in her eyes is practically on fire. I love seeing her like this. She's not hiding or making note of the quickest exit plan—something I've noticed she does quite often.

No, this Shay is bright and genuine and so damn beautiful I have to kiss her. It's a necessity. I taste her smile when our lips meet, her flavor coursing through me and spiking my veins, making me hard as a fucking rock.

"Keep kissing me like that and we might not make it to dinner," she whispers when we break apart, her cheeks flushed and lips swollen. I want to say fuck it to dinner and throw her over my shoulder and carry her off to bed, but she's not ready for that yet. I see it in her eyes.

"We have plenty of time for everything, sunshine," I say, kissing her on the forehead. I nearly groan when she pouts, but I manage to stay the course. Barely.

I step away from her and rummage around in my cupboards for something halfway decent to make. The only thing I have is bread and Cup O'Noodles. Shay walks up behind me, trying unsuccessfully to swallow down her laugh.

"Well, the cat's out of the bag," I sigh defeatedly. "I can't cook to save my life and I've been eating like a bachelor since I moved in."

Shay graces me with another one of her brilliant smiles. "It's good to know you're not perfect," she teases.

"Oh, I'm certainly not perfect. Let's get that cleared up right away."

She just shrugs and spins around again, making her way toward the fridge. "You're pretty perfect to me," she murmurs so quietly I almost don't hear her. Damn, this woman. She's far too good for me.

I continue searching the kitchen for food while Shay digs around in the fridge. I find a can of peaches and about twenty cans of tomato soup in the walk-in pantry from the previous tenants.

"Is the soup still good?" Shay asks from behind me.

"For another two years."

"Great! Okay, I've got dinner handled. You pick something to watch."

I turn around and grin at my girl, the excited look on her face enough to make me melt for her completely. She's giving me another piece of herself. Every smile, teasing glance, sultry word, and lighthearted laugh binds her heart closer to mine.

"It hardly seems fair to invite you over for dinner, only to have you cook for us."

"I don't mind! It was kind of fun figuring out what I could make out of random ingredients. Now go on and pick a movie or something." She shoos me out of my own kitchen, making me chuckle.

"Yes, ma'am," I joke.

"And it better not be one of your movies!" she adds, making me laugh even more.

"What, you're sick of me already?"

"No, I just like the real thing better." My girl winks at me, and yeah, you're goddamn right my dick is making my pants uncomfortably tight. I can't come up with a clever response, seeing as all the blood has changed course and now resides in my aching groin.

Ten minutes later, Shay walks into the living room with a tray of food. I jump up to help her, smiling when I see two bowls of tomato soup and a stack of grilled cheese sandwiches cut diagonally and arranged in a spiraling tower.

"I want points for resourcefulness, presentation, and getting dinner on the table in a timely manner," she informs me.

"Baby, you can have all the points you want. What are they counting toward?" I ask, pulling her down into my lap once the tray is on the coffee table. Shay gasps and then giggles as she gets situated.

"That's for me to know, and you to find out."

"Is that right?" I growl softly, kissing the back of her neck. Shay nods her head slightly, and I trail kisses over her shoulder, unable to keep my lips off of her.

She giggles and squirms in my arms. "That tickles!"

I smirk and rub my stubbled chin into the crook of her neck, making her laugh harder. The sound fills the room and echoes in my head, settling deep in my chest. God, it's beautiful. She's beautiful.

As much as I want to hold her right here forever, we do need to eat. I get her situated next to me and hand her a plate with her bowl of soup and a sandwich before grabbing my own.

"Okay, now before digging in, let me tell you about the feast I've prepared," she says in all seriousness. Well, except for the small little grin flickering in her eyes. I love this playful side of her. "Here we have piping hot pureed tomatoes seasoned with more additives and preservatives than you can shake a stick at." I crack a grin, but swallow down my laughter, urging her to continue. "And to the left of your tomato puree, you'll see my signature three-cheese toasted sandwich."

"I had three kinds of cheese in my fridge?"

"Well, *cheese* is stretching the truth a bit. You had Kraft American Cheese product, shredded mozzarella, and dried, crumbled parmesan in a plastic shaker." Her nose scrunches up after she lists my apparently offensive not-cheeses, which is just about the cutest thing I've ever seen. "But don't you worry. This meal will be delicious. I know the chef."

With that, Shay dips the corner of her sandwich into the soup and takes a big bite. The grin on her face was well worth the slight embarrassment of not having anything substantial, let alone impressive, to cook. I dig in as well, pleasantly surprised at how good everything is.

We scarf down dinner and get settled in for the movie I picked. It's an old Danny Kaye movie, which Shay immediately loves. I figured it was a safe bet since I don't know what kinds of things trigger her anxiety. I got my woman to laugh and smile and flirt with me; no way in hell I want to ruin that.

Shay curls up next to me, resting her head on my shoulder. I move my arm, wrapping it around her waist and tucking her into my side. She sighs contentedly and snuggles closer, laying her head down on my chest. I inhale her sugary, jasmine scent and take a second to appreciate the weight of her body pressed against mine.

It takes all of twenty minutes for Shay to doze off. I don't mind. In fact, I love that she felt comfortable enough to fall asleep at my place, in my arms, no less. I reach behind her and grab the blanket that was always just for show, spreading it out over her and tucking her in. This night is nothing like I planned. It's infinitely better.

Chapter 6

I'm the warmest, coziest, most relaxed I've ever been, but something woke me up. I try ignoring it, snuggling down deeper into the safety of the blanket on top of me and the furnace beneath me.

Wait. Furnace?

"Shay, sweetheart, your phone is going off," a voice whispers. I feel something stroking my back, waking me up gently. After a few moments, my senses come back to me. I'm in Weston's penthouse, sprawled out on top of him while he rubs my back.

Oh God, I fell asleep on him? Did I drool?

My eyes snap open at the thought and immediately look down, relieved to see Weston's shirt is drool-free. "Sorry," I mumble, trying to untangle myself from him.

Weston pulls me back down on top of him and kisses the tip of my nose. "There's nothing to be sorry about," he says softly before pressing a kiss to my forehead. I sigh and curl up on his chest, fluttering my eyes closed. I can't help it. He feels too good to move. And then my phone rings again, startling me out of his arms. "I wouldn't have woken you up, but it's gone off a few times throughout the evening."

I nod sleepily and manage to stand up, though I take that blanket with me, wrapping it around my shoulders. Weston grunts, making me laugh a bit, despite the growing knot in my stomach. It's nearly nine p.m., I'm not sure who would be calling me. It's not like I have many other friends besides Ainsley, but she knows I have my date tonight.

Gathering my purse up from where I left it on the side table, I dig around and grab my phone. I have one missed call from an unknown number and three missed calls from Ainsley. Both left voicemails. I don't want to check them, but I know I'll be anxious about it until I hear what they say.

"This message is for Shay Sullivan. This is Officer Boswell with the Washington State Penitentiary..."

I listen to the rest of the message, but it sounds like it's coming from a tin can. Sean got out early. He's out *right now*. Holy shit.

With shaky fingers, I tap to listen to the next message. It's Ainsley, telling me she also got a call from Officer Boswell. She was there the night everything happened and he threatened her as well. I hate that she got caught up in my drama, but Ainsley is nothing if not resilient. Her voicemail was all concern for me, of course, and nothing about herself. I really do have the best friend in the whole world.

I manage to send Ainsley a text, though it takes me much longer than it should. I keep mistyping words, my hands are shaking so badly.

"Shay? Baby, what's wrong?"

Weston is right beside me, his voice so soft and worried it makes more tears stream down my face. He reaches out for me, but then hesitates like he's not sure if I want to be touched right now. Normally, I wouldn't, but I find myself longing for the safety I've only ever found in his arms.

I lean against Weston and let him haul me into his lap, blanket and all. We're both still on the floor, but neither one of us makes a move to get up. "I'm right here, sunshine," he whispers, holding me close. "You're safe right here. You're safe with me."

"I know," I manage to squeak out in between sniffles. And I do. Weston has only ever made me feel comfortable and seen, truly seen for the first time in so long. It's not him I'm worried about. It's me. I can't get used to this kind of thing. I can't depend on Weston. Not when he's going to be leaving me in a few weeks. The thought makes me cry all over again. God, I'm a mess.

"Let me get you settled in bed. You can stay in one of the extra rooms."

I immediately shake my head no, but I can't bring myself to leave the warmth of his embrace. "I can't," I whisper.

"Why not?"

"I just... I can't," I say again.

How do I explain the man who's haunted my dreams for years? What would he think of me if he knew how weak I was? How weak I still am? I was so stupid to think auditioning for a play would somehow erase the last three years. Erase the fear that's constantly tugging at the corners of my mind. Erase the panic always simmering just beneath the surface. The sleepless nights and manic days, wondering if I'll ever truly feel safe again. I thought maybe I was past all that, if the last month of being around Weston was any indication. But now I know I'm no stronger than I was that night all those years ago. One phone call brought me right back to that alley...

"Okay, sweetheart. It's okay. Breathe for me," he says so softly it nearly breaks my heart. I rest my head against his chest, feeling it rise and fall evenly with each breath, and listen to the steady beat of his heart.

Weston doesn't pressure me to talk or try to convince me to stay, though I can tell he wants to. Instead, he's giving me control. He's letting me decide what I share and when. It's just one more way this man is breaking down my defenses. As much as I want to tell him everything, I'm scared to ruin what we have. This was the perfect evening up until the phone calls.

I don't know how long I stay curled up on his lap, but eventually, I know it's time to go. Any longer in his arms and I may give in and let him take every last piece of my pain and fear. But for how long?

I can tell he doesn't want to let me go, but once again, he lets me take the lead. We don't say anything as I gather up my things and take the elevator down to the parking garage. Weston holds my hand in the car, but we still haven't spoken a word. What is there to say? He wants to know my secrets and I can't tell him. The longer the silence goes on, however, I worry that I've upset him.

As if reading my thoughts, Weston squeezes my hand and gently rubs his thumb over my knuckles. "You'll tell me when you're ready, sunshine. And I'll be right here to listen." All I can do is nod my head and tighten my grip on his hand, not wanting to let go of this man, but needing to all the same.

I'm barely keeping it together by the time Weston pulls into the parking lot of my apartment building. We sit in his idling car for a beat too long, the quiet, still night air hanging heavy with unspoken questions and answers.

Weston is the first one to get out of the car, coming around to my door and helping me out. He tucks me into his side as he walks me to my door. I fidget, not sure how to end the night. I'm sure it was nothing like he expected. I mean, the man had reservations at Purple and I made him go back to his place to eat canned tomato soup before falling asleep on him, and then I had a breakdown.

The last of the confidence I felt earlier in the evening evaporates, leaving me impossibly exhausted. I look down at where our fingers are intertwined and then back up into his green eyes full of worry.

"I'm sorry," I say lamely. "I was having the best night before..."

Weston cups my face in both of his hands, holding me so gently as his deep, emerald eyes search mine. He leans down, capturing my lips in the most tender kiss imaginable. We've had claiming kisses, desperate kisses, and explosive kisses, but none were like this. He takes his time, sipping from me like he's trying to savor every moment we're together.

I give in to him, leaning against his solid frame and letting him support me. Weston breaks our kiss, pressing his lips to my forehead and breathing me in. "There's nothing to apologize for," he finally whispers. "I had the best night with you, too, Shay. I can't wait to have lots more just like it."

I nod against his lips before untangling myself and fumbling for my keys. I turn and look at the man who is undoing me piece by piece, wanting to say so many things, but lacking the courage. It's a familiar feeling, but I hate it all the same. Helpless. Stuck in my thoughts. Unable to take a leap and follow through.

Weston doesn't press me for any more words, which is good, because I don't have any to give him. Instead, he gives me a small smile and watches me go inside. I close the door and slump against it, burying my face in my hands.

I don't love the idea of spending the night alone, but it's my own damn fault. On the other hand, it gives me space to process the wave of memories and emotions scratching at the surface.

I don't bother washing my face or brushing my teeth, opting instead to crawl under my blankets, fully clothed. It takes all the energy I have to turn off the light. My phone buzzes a split second later, making me jump out of my skin. Relief floods through me when I see it's a text from Weston.

Get some sleep, sunshine. I promise I'll keep you safe.

My first instinct is to brush it off as an empty promise, or at least a promise he can't possibly fulfill. But something pushes through the fear. Something close to hope. Something almost like peace. How long has it been since I felt at ease? And how am I feeling it right now, when my worst nightmare has come true?

My eyelids grow heavy and my mind drifts off before I can come up with any answers. I didn't think I'd be able to sleep at all tonight, but I can't keep my eyes open any longer. Maybe this was all a terrible dream. Maybe when I wake up again, I'll be back on Weston's couch, snuggled into his arms. I swear I can almost feel his presence as exhaustion pulls me under.

***

I can't believe what I'm seeing. I close my front door and then open it again, positive that I made it up. But he's still there. Weston. He's sitting in the hallway outside my door, asleep. Surely, he wasn't out here all night, right? That's crazy. Why would he do that?

He wakes with a start, his eyes flying open as he jumps to his feet and looks around, surveying for danger. Only when he's satisfied that there's no threat does he turn his gaze toward me.

"Shay," he breathes out, relief flooding his features. The man has bags under his bloodshot eyes, his hair is a wild mess, and his back and neck have to be killing him from sitting outside my door all night, but none of that seems to matter to him as he gives me an easy smile. He's undeniably gorgeous, even in his disheveled state.

"Weston... why... what are you doing here?"

He takes a step closer to me, his eyes never leaving mine. "I promised I wouldn't let anything happen to you," he says with a shrug, as if it's obvious. "You felt more comfortable in your own space, and I respect that, but I couldn't just leave you all alone, crying in your apartment."

"I don't know what to say," I whisper.

"You don't have to say anything. How did you sleep?"

"How did *I* sleep? How did *you* sleep?"

"I've slept in worse places," he says with a grin that doesn't reach his eyes. I furrow my brow, not sure I understood him right. Hollywood royalty used to sleep in worse places than the hallway of an apartment building? "I'll tell you all about it later. For now, I need a change of clothes and some coffee."

"Let me get your coffee. It's literally the least I can do to thank you. God, I never even said that. Thank you. I couldn't figure out why I was able to sleep at all last night, but now I know. I felt you." I stare at him, part in awe, part in confusion, before I realize I probably sound like an idiot.

"Never thank me for taking care of you," he tells me softly, drawing me in for a hug. "That being said, I'd never turn down a coffee date with you."

I nod, burying my face into the side of his neck as he wraps his arms around me. I want to tell him everything. Just not right now. I have to find the right moment, and this one is too pure to ruin it with my past.

"Didn't anyone recognize you?" I blurt out awkwardly. "I mean, you're Weston freaking Cooper Haze."

He laughs, the rumble in his chest soothing me and making me smile. He has a beautiful laugh. I don't think I've ever heard anything like it.

"One guy did a double take, but he shrugged it off. I'm sure the whole loitering in the hallway thing threw him off track."

"But I mean, who could ignore you?"

"I could say the same for you," he says with a grin. I try to smile back, but my gut twists a bit at his words.

"Yeah, that's the problem," I mumble, my hand automatically going to my head to make sure my hair is pulled back. It's subconscious at this point, my need to tame my hair and make it as least noticeable as possible. It's always brought me a lot of attention. Not many people are born with hair so blonde it's nearly white. But I can't bring myself to dye it. I used to love my hair. I guess I always hoped one day I'd be comfortable enough to show it off again.

Weston carefully removes my hand from where I had it to cover my hair and kisses my palm so sweetly. "You're stunning. And I'm damn lucky I get to be the guy to prove that to you."

I can't hide the smile on my face. "Is that a line from one of your movies?" I tease. The sparkle in his eye almost makes me forget about everything that happened last night.

"I'd never reuse old lines on you, sunshine."

"Same," I tell him with a cheeky grin.

This makes Weston laugh again. I can't help but join in. Who would have thought I could laugh and smile after the last twelve hours? Only Weston can bring out this side of me. I've missed it. I wonder what other things he could make me feel...

Chapter 7

Weston

"Weston! Let's talk about the scene transition after act two," Reggie says, making me roll my eyes.

Opening night is just under two weeks away, and the director seems to need a lot of reassurance that everything is going to be okay. I know it will because I've done at least eighty percent of the directing myself. Oddly enough, I don't mind. In fact, I kind of enjoyed it. Maybe even more than acting.

Reggie calls for me again and I sigh, resigned to my fate. I look around the theater for Shay, but I only get a glimpse of her enchanting ice-blonde hair before she follows one of the makeup artists backstage.

My chest grows tight at her beauty, but also at her pain. I can't stop thinking about our date night. Her eyes sparked to life when she was cooking and cuddling with me. Her smile shined so radiantly, and her laughter filled my penthouse with joy and warmth.

And then she got those phone calls.

I held her in my arms, silently begging her to let me in, to let me see her, all of her, and ease her worries. But she was in no state of mind to be confessing anything. I felt her fear, her helplessness, her agony. The longer I cradled her in my arms, the more of her pain I absorbed. It nearly crippled me. I don't know how Shay walks around with all of that weighing on her shoulders, every second of every day.

All I want in the whole world is to carry her burden for her, but I know I can't. I can share it with her, let her know she's not alone, but my girl doesn't need a savior. Just like Seneca, she's stronger than she thinks. I can't wait for the day she demands my love for real, and not just as a line in a play.

Shay has been extra skittish since she got those phone calls. Every little noise seems to rattle her these days. I hate that for her. I've tried asking about the calls in roundabout ways the last two weeks, but she shuts down on me every single time.

Reggie clears his throat, pulling me from my thoughts. He looks annoyed, but then again, so do I. If not for Shay, this whole thing would have been a completely miserable disaster. But now? Well, now I'd work with a hundred Reggie's and deal with all the fangirls a thousand times over as long as it led me straight to my sunshine.

I go over the script with Reggie and reassure his fragile ego that everything is going to be fine. My phone rings, *thank god*, and I step away to answer it.

"Hello?"

"Weston?"

I pull the phone away from my ear and stare at the screen. It's a number I don't recognize. The voice, however, is unmistakable.

"Rider?" I question, still not believing it's my oldest friend.

"Damn straight, pretty boy," he says with a rough chuckle.

I smirk at his nickname for me. He came up with it the second that agent handed me her card on the construction site. "How the hell are you? I haven't heard from you in ages. Someone told me you ended up in the slammer, but that doesn't sound like you."

Rider heaves a heavy sigh, and I can just picture him wiping a hand down his face before slapping his knee. Sure enough, a second later, I hear a smack.

"It's a long, fucked up story, but yeah. I was locked up for five years, two months, and fourteen days."

"Jesus," I mutter. I want to know everything that happened, but I can tell my friend isn't up for reliving everything right now. I know we'll talk about it when he's ready.

"Just got out last week," he continues. "I'm back with the Savage Saints MC. They kept my old job for me at the body shop and set me up with an apartment behind the clubhouse. I've finally started to settle in and wanted to check up on friends I lost contact with while serving time."

"It's good to hear your voice," I tell him truthfully.

"Yeah? The Hollywood elite not doing it for you anymore?"

"You have no idea," I grunt. "Turns out you're not the only one with a wild streak."

"That right? What kind of trouble have you gotten yourself into?"

"Nothing too serious, but my PR team has an aneurysm everytime my name pops up in the headlines, so I'm hiding out in Seattle, working on a small theater production."

"Sounds miserable."

I chuckle, thinking back to when I first heard the news. "It was. Until I met my future wife."

"What?! Hold on, how the hell did that happen? Wife? Last time I checked, you were in a messy on-again/off-again thing with that shrew of a singer."

I cringe at the thought of ever spending time with Teresa, then let out a chuckle at Rider's description of my ex.

"Man, I don't know what the hell I was thinking with her. I wasn't. We were pushed together by our fans and agents, and neither one of us gave enough of a shit to stop it. After our final break-up, she made it her life's mission to drag my career down right along with hers."

"Sounds about right."

"I was... lost for a while, I guess. Not because I was grieving our relationship. Fuck no. I just realized after a decade and a half in Hollywood, I still don't know who I am. I've played countless roles, had a personal shopper to dress me in the latest trends, earned enough money to buy anything and everything, but the most authentic I've ever felt was working on that construction site with you."

Silence stretches between us, and I start to regret being so vulnerable.

"Not that my problems are anything compared to what you've been through the last few years," I follow-up.

"None of that shit," Rider rasps. "You've done some soul searching. Ain't nothing to diminish. I've done some similar searching myself lately."

Before I can ask a follow-up question, I hear someone shout my friend's name in the background.

"Ah, shit, gotta go. We got an unexpected and unwelcome visit from the cops," Rider growls. "Probably checking up on me."

"Thanks for calling, Rider. I mean it. We need to catch up when the police aren't knocking at your door."

Rider grumbles a string of cuss words before saying goodbye and hanging up.

I shake my head, but can't keep the smile off my face. As cheesy as it sounds, getting that call feels like a sign. It's time to go back to my roots, back to a time I actually liked myself. What that means for my career, I have no idea. As long as Shay is with me, it doesn't matter where I end up.

Wandering around the set, I peek into the back room where they're doing hair and makeup for the dress rehearsal, searching for Shay. She's sitting in front of a vanity mirror while someone standing behind her says something. I see Shay's face in the mirror, her eyes going wide before she furrows her brow and shakes her head no.

The woman standing behind her starts touching Shay's hair, and I see her visibly flinch. Clenching my fists at my sides, I bite back the urge to yell at the lady who caused my girl distress. I swallow down my anger, not wanting to make a scene, but I can't help storming over to her.

"Shay," I nearly growl, kicking myself when she jumps. "I need you for a minute." I don't bother looking at the hair and makeup lady as I grab Shay's hand and lead her out of the room. She visibly relaxes the farther away we walk.

I want to ask her what it is about her hair that she's so self-conscious about, but I know she'll tell me when she's ready. Or, at least I hope she will. I know Shay trusts me, and I know she feels safe around me. That's enough for now.

"What's up?" she asks once I've guided her to a secluded hallway.

I turn toward her, cupping the back of her neck and drawing her in for a kiss. Shay melts against me, her muscles finally relaxing completely as I slip my tongue between her lips. I continue holding the back of her neck while my other hand wraps around her waist, pressing her body closer to mine. She gasps softly, then tips her head back and moans as I grind my aching cock against her core.

"It's been too damn long since I've tasted you," I whisper before kissing her again. I nip at her bottom lip, pulling it through my teeth and then diving into her sweetness.

"Wow," she breathes out once we break apart, both of us panting. I grin at her adorable response, resting my forehead against hers. Shay closes her eyes like she's trying to hang on to this moment and remember it. Doesn't she know I'll give her moments like this every single day?

Wait. *Does* she know that? We haven't talked about what happens after the play is over in just under two weeks. I didn't want to scare her off with the intensity of my feelings, but I see now I've only made her doubt what we have by letting her think I'm leaving soon. Not a fucking chance.

This is neither the time nor the place to have this discussion, however.

"Wow," I say back, pressing a kiss to her forehead. "Come over tonight. We can run lines."

Shay tips her head back and gives me a playful little smirk. Jesus, what that does to me. I'll cherish every single one of her smiles. It fills me up with inexplicable pride that I can bring that out in her.

"Is that what the kids are calling it these days?"

"I don't know what you're talking about," I murmur, brushing my lips against hers.

"Mmhm," she says softly, tilting her head up and closing her eyes. Her perfectly pouty lips part slightly, making my dick strain against my zipper.

"My intentions are honorable," I whisper, trailing kisses down her neck.

"Shame."

I groan, gripping her hips and walking her backward until she's right up against the wall. I lean into her, pinning her to the wall with my body. She lets out a whimper and writhes against me, the desperate sound making me feral. I want all of her sounds. I want to hear her moan in ecstasy, cry out as I sink into her, and shout my name as she comes.

My hands slide down her curves, gripping her ass and kneading the soft flesh. Shay wraps her arms around my neck and clings to me as I claim her mouth in a searing kiss. My right hand drifts down to her thigh and I grip her there, guiding her leg up to wrap around my hips. She follows my lead, allowing me to open her up even more as I grind my thickness against her.

I know the second I rub against her clit. Her entire body trembles and her nails dig into my scalp, the sting only amplifying the pleasure coursing through me.

Regrettably, I have to tear my mouth away from hers so I can fill my lungs with air. She does the same, leaning her head against the wall and closing her eyes.

"I'll run lines with you anytime," she says, her voice slightly slurred. I groan and nearly kiss her again, but I manage to control myself. If I kiss her again, I swear I might come in my goddamn pants. We still have three hours of rehearsal left, so that would not be an ideal situation.

As much as it pains me, I set her leg down and step away from her, running my hands through my hair. Shay leans against the wall, still a little unsteady from our kisses. God, this woman is so responsive. I can't wait to get her naked and run my tongue over every inch of her perfect body.

"Tonight," I grunt, making Shay laugh.

"Tonight," she repeats before standing on her tiptoes and kissing my cheek. I try to get her to kiss me for real, but she has more restraint than I do. Shay spins out of my arms and gives me the sexiest, most wicked little grin. Damn, this woman is going to be the death of me.

***

The last few hours of rehearsal lasted at least a year. Every minute felt like a day. We wrapped up fifteen minutes ago and I managed to squeak by, under Reggie's radar. No way am I spending another hour discussing scenes and acting techniques with the insufferable kiss ass.

I find Shay gathering her things from the lockers in the back and pause for a moment to appreciate her beauty. She has the most delicate features; high cheekbones, full lips, and big, soulful brown eyes that make her look like a fucking porcelain doll. I'm drawn toward her, my feet moving on their own, wanting to be closer to this angel.

"Hey, sunshine," I murmur, trying to make my voice soft so I don't startle her. Shay spins around with the biggest smile on her face. It hits me right in the chest, making me gasp quietly for air.

"Hey," she says, biting her bottom lip. "Ready to... run lines?" Her eyebrow quirks up, her smile turning mischievous.

"I'm ready for whatever you are."

Her cheeks flush bright pink, making my already semi-hard dick lengthen and swell in my jeans. I love making her blush. I hope to see how far down it goes and if the color matches her nipples. Clearing my head of those thoughts, I reach out for her hand and lace our fingers together. Shay squeezes my hand and lets me lead her out to my car.

I help her inside, buckling her seatbelt and placing a sweet kiss on her cute little nose. I don't even care how much of a sappy motherfucker that makes me. Her soft, dreamy smile is worth it.

We're about halfway to my place when the sky opens up and pours buckets of rain. Seattle is known for the rain, but from what I've gathered, it hardly ever downpours. Shay grips her seatbelt, her knuckles turning white. I slow down and take her hand in mine, rubbing my thumb over her knuckles in the way I know she likes. I like it, too. I like that I can calm her down, even just a little bit.

It's still coming down heavily when we pull into my temporary apartment, the sound almost deafening as it echoes throughout the parking garage. I hop out of the car and help Shay out, tucking her into my side as we make our way to the elevator. I'm practically carrying her. I'd scoop her up in my arms, but I get the feeling she might be embarrassed by that.

"I can walk, you know," she mumbles, though she doesn't step away from me.

"I know. You can do anything you want. I just like you by my side, if that's alright."

Shay tries to hide her smile, but I see it anyway. As soon as we're in the elevator, I pull Shay in front of me, her back to my front. My hands slide down to her hips, gripping her and pulling her closer to me. I know she feels how hard I am for her. The little minx grinds her ass against me, making me growl as I slip my hands just barely under her shirt.

Jesus, her skin is so soft. Shay's breath catches in her throat as she leans her head back, resting on my shoulder. She's opening herself up to me, surrendering to my touch, my desire. I'm about to spin her around and kiss the air from her lungs, but the elevator stops and the doors open.

I take a deep breath to calm myself down. It's a struggle to keep my hands off her, but I don't want to push her too far. I get the feeling my sunshine doesn't have a lot of experience and fuck if that doesn't make me want to show her every single way I can make her come. I want to be the one to give her pleasure so deep, so drugging, she never wants to leave.

That thought isn't helping.

"Do you want something to drink?" I ask, instead of bending her over the couch and taking her from behind.

"Yeah, water's fine." We share a lingering look, one that stirs something deep inside me. Yes, I'm turned on beyond belief and harder than I've ever been in my whole damn life, but it's more than that. She's precious. A rare beauty, inside and out, though she has no idea. I want everything with her. I want everything from her. I'll give her all of me in return. Hell, she already has me. I'm hers.

When I get back to the living room with two glasses of water, Shay is sitting on the couch with her legs tucked underneath her, flipping through the script. She looks comfortable in my space, like she's lived with me for years, and this is something we do every night.

I can't help myself. I set the glasses down and sit next to her, pulling her onto my lap so she's straddling me. Shay gasps and then giggles at the sudden movement. She steadies herself with her hands on my shoulders.

God, she's beautiful.

"Um, thanks," Shay whispers. Oops. I didn't mean to say that out loud, but the way I feel about her is no secret.

I lean closer to her, ghosting my nose and lips down her neck and breathing in her sugary jasmine scent. She hums in approval, the breathy little sound going straight to my cock. Shay rocks her hips against me, though I don't think she's even aware she's doing it.

I groan and nip at her pulse point, resisting the urge to suck and bite her skin until my mark is there. I've never had such a primal, caveman need to claim someone as my own. Everyone needs to know Shay Sullivan is fucking *mine.*

"Weren't we going to run lines?" she asks, tilting her head to the side to give me better access.

"Definitely," I murmur, scraping my teeth along her throat, groaning when she squeezes her thighs around my hips. I feel her heat as Shay writhes in my lap, rubbing herself against my jean-covered cock. "We should get right on that."

Shay nods her head but makes no move to get off of me. I slowly slide my hands up her torso, testing the waters to see what she's comfortable with.

When I reach her gorgeous, perfect breasts, I can't help but cup them in my large hands. I rub my thumbs against her nipples, both hard little peaks just begging for attention. A shiver runs down her spine and she gasps like she didn't know that would feel so good. She's killing me here. I want to rip off her clothes and lick every inch of her body.

"Yeah," she whispers in the least convincing voice ever. "We should... get right... on that." Her voice is nearly a moan by the time she finishes her sentence.

My hands roam all over her body, tracing her soft curves as I kiss my woman breathless. Without thinking about it, my hands find their way to her hair, which is pulled back in a conservative bun, like it always is. Shay stiffens in my arms, and I drop my hands back down to her hips, keeping her anchored to me. I'm not sure why she's so sensitive about her hair. It's certainly not the first time she's shied away from me, and apparently from anyone who draws attention to it, if the lady from earlier today is any indication.

I cup the sides of her neck, holding her gently as I stare into those deep brown eyes of hers. "Do you trust me, sunshine?" I whisper, searching her face for the truth.

Shay slowly nods her head, though there's more than a little apprehension in her gaze. Without breaking eye contact, I slide one hand to the nape of her neck, my fingers finding the clip that's holding her hair back. Shay closes her eyes and tips her head back, urging me to continue. I know this is a big deal for her, even if I don't have all the answers yet as to why.

I take the clip and bobby pins out of her hair, watching in awe as the lightest, most beautiful blonde hair tumbles down around her back and shoulders. It's longer than I thought it would be, reaching just past her mouth-watering tits.

I comb my fingers through her long locks, satisfied beyond belief when a sweet sigh escapes her lips. I can't take my eyes off her. She was mesmerizing before, but now she's otherworldly. My girl is pure magic and sunshine. There's no other way to describe her.

Tangling my hands in her hair, I tug gently and tilt her head back so I can nuzzle into the side of her neck. "Thank you for letting me see you, sweetheart," I murmur. I'm not sure why I said that, but it feels right, like it's exactly what she needed to hear.

"Thank you for everything."

I'm about to ask what she means, but there's a bright flash of lighting, followed by a deafening clap of thunder. The lights flicker and then go out completely. I love the idea of spending the evening in the dark, exploring Shay's luscious body, but those thoughts die in an instant when she lets out a little cry and clings to me, burying her face into the side of my neck.

"It's alright. I'm sure it'll kick back on soon," I say softly while rubbing her back. She nods but tightens her hold on me. We sit in silence for a few minutes, waiting for the power to return. Shay is trembling in my arms and once again I get the overwhelming urge to end whoever made her afraid of the dark.

When it's clear there's no backup generator coming on, I decide to call the front desk. They have someone on staff twenty-four seven. I move Shay off my lap and stand up to grab my phone. Shay jumps up with me and fists the back of my shirt. I feel the paralyzing fear rolling off of her in waves.

I turn my phone's flashlight on to provide some light, then bend down and grab Shay's purse. "Want to find your phone, baby?" I ask gently. "You can turn your flashlight on, too, okay?"

She nods and reaches out for her purse, but her hands are shaking so badly I think she might drop it. I swallow down the anger and heartache, vowing to fill her life with so much light and joy that it drowns out the darkness.

I hold out the purse for her, opening it up so she can dig through. Once she has it, she immediately turns the flashlight on, clutching it in her hand like a weapon. I grab my phone and dial the front desk while wrapping my free arm around Shay and holding her close.

"I've got you," I whisper, placing a kiss on the crown of her head. I call Larry, the overnight front desk guy, on his cell and ask about an update. Unfortunately, the storm knocked down a few massive trees, cutting down power lines across the city and blowing out not only the main power grid for our area but the backup one as well. His best guess for when it would be fixed is sometime tomorrow. I thank him and hang up, still holding my sunshine close.

"Wh-what'd he s-say?" she stutters out.

"Power's out until tomorrow at least."

"Oh no." It's barely a whisper, but the lost, helpless tone in her voice breaks me deep inside.

"You're safe here, Shay. I promise. Stay with me."

"I… I don't know. I should call my neighbor and see if there's power in our building. If there is, I can just go back there."

I need to find a way to convince her to stay without scaring her off completely. There's no way I'm letting her leave. Not in the middle of a storm and certainly not while the power is out and she's scared out of her mind.

If she needs to call her building manager, that's fine. I'm positive the power is out there as well. And if it's not? I'll take her back. And stay the night parked outside of her door again if that's what she needs.

I nod my head and give her a little space to make her call. She grabs my hand to keep me next to her. I hate that she's afraid, but I love knowing I'm her anchor, her safe place.

"Lindsey, this is Shay from unit 5B. I was calling to see if... It's out there, too?" She sighs, her shoulders dropping. "Not until tomorrow, huh?" Shay looks up at me, a tentative smile on her face. Was she hoping for an excuse to stay the night? She doesn't need one. I'm hoping to spend every night with her from now on. "Looks like you're stuck with me," she says once she hangs up.

"Lucky me." I tuck some of her hair behind her ear, letting my fingers trail down her slightly wavy, soft as silk locks.

"You might not be saying that when I can't sleep," she mumbles under her breath.

"I'll be right here," I remind her. Another flash of lightning lights up the sky, and Shay covers her ears right before the clap of thunder tears through the sky. It's so powerful it rattles the windows. "Let's get you to bed, baby." Shay nods and lets me scoop her up in my arms and carry her to the master bedroom.

I grab a pair of my boxers and a t-shirt for her to slip on. As much as I want to peel her out of her clothes and dress her myself—or, preferably, leave her naked—I have enough of my wits about me to know how incredibly inappropriate that is right now.

I'm about to leave to give her some privacy, but she calls out to me right as I reach the door.

"Wait. Could you stay? Maybe just turn around?"

"Of course. Whatever you need."

I turn my back to her, trying not to imagine what she looks like underneath her conservative clothing. I've felt her curves, tasted her lips, and dreamt about the wicked things I'm going to do to her. Again, I chastise myself for having these thoughts while she's clearly scared. Though maybe I could provide her with a distraction...

I feel her walk up behind me and wrap her arms around my waist before burying her head into my back. I rest my hands over hers and soak in the love she's giving me. Maybe *she* doesn't know it yet, but I do. She's in this as much as I am, but it'll take time for her to believe it's real. We're real.

Eventually, I turn around and guide her over to the bed, pulling the covers back for her. Once she's settled in, I quickly strip down to my boxers and crawl in behind her, spooning around her much smaller body.

"I'm sorry I'm such a mess," Shay finally whispers. I tighten my hold on her and kiss the back of her neck.

"Shay, I know you don't understand this yet, but one day you'll trust that all I want to do is take care of you. You're not a burden. You're not a mess. You're mine."

She inhales sharply but then relaxes. I can feel some of the stress and tension drain away as she snuggles deeper into my embrace. Her peace is short-lived, however, as another clap of thunder shatters the silence.

"See? I told you that you'd regret inviting me to stay." I can tell she wanted to make a joke, but there's too much insecurity in her tone to pull it off.

"Never, sunshine. I'll never regret spending time with you. But maybe I could help... *distract* you from the storm?" I didn't mean for the words to slip out, but god, I hope she says yes.

I swear to Christ I can feel her body heat up at my words.

"What did you have in mind?" she asks breathlessly while wiggling her ass further into me. I groan when she brushes up against my erection.

"Do you trust me?" I ask her for the second time tonight as I slip my hand beneath the too big shirt of mine that she's wearing.

"With all of me."

I growl softly at her response, feeling like the fucking king of the world.

"Then relax and let me take your mind off everything."

"Yes, please." Her breathy reply is my undoing.

Chapter 8

Shay

Weston spreads his hand out over my stomach, softly caressing my skin. That simple touch makes my pussy throb and my skin break out into goosebumps. I should be embarrassed about being afraid of the dark and the thunderstorm, but God, I can't think of anything else when his hands are on me, which I suppose is the point.

"You're so soft," Weston murmurs as he pulls me closer to him. Every single inch of his body is rock hard, from the defined muscles on his chest and abs to his thick cock digging into my ass. It feels so good being pressed against him while he continues to explore my body with gentle, yet scorching, touches.

I arch my back when he cups my breast and glides his thumb against my pebbled nipple. Weston growls softly and grinds his erection against me. He kisses the back of my neck then nips at the sensitive spot just below my ear. I can't help but whimper when he scrapes his teeth along the same spot like he wants to devour me. I want him to. I want him to take what I've never offered to anyone else. Maybe not tonight, but I've never even considered it with anyone else before.

He tugs at my shirt, managing to lift it up and over my head with little to no help from me. Weston squeezes my breasts and pinches one nipple, then the other. He grunts something about perfect little tits, but I hardly hear him over the overwhelming sensations he's causing in me.

Weston slides his hand down my torso, his fingers dancing along the edge of his boxers that I'm wearing. The featherlight touch drives me crazy. He's teasing me, making me squirm, making me want so much more. I've never been this needy, this desperate, this...wet. God, I'm so, so incredibly turned on right now. I always am around Weston, but right now I *ache* for him.

He slips just the tips of his fingers beneath the elastic waistband, making me gasp at the sudden rush of arousal shooting through me.

Every nerve ending spikes with pleasure, causing more wetness to coat the insides of my thighs.

"This okay, sunshine?" Weston asks softly, his voice tinged with the same desperate need I feel.

"Yes," I whimper. "Please."

He groans and wastes no time shoving the boxers down my thighs. I wiggle and help him remove them completely as needy little whimpers fall from my lips, my desire growing each second his fingers aren't inside me.

Once I'm completely naked, Weston runs his hand across my bare skin, leaving a trail of fire in its wake. Finally, fucking *finally,* he dips one finger into my slit and strokes me. I cry out when he circles my clit with his calloused fingers. My core pulses and clenches up, and I swear I'm already right at the edge of total bliss.

"So wet for me," he grunts, circling my opening with the pad of his finger. I buck my hips and grind down on his hand, unable to control my movements. Weston teases my pulsing little hole, not quite entering me. How does that feel so good? I wiggle my hips, trying to get him to do...something. I don't know. I just need more.

He runs his fingers up and down my slit, gathering up my juices and rubbing my clit until I'm moaning uncontrollably. I'm right there, so close I'm shaking. So close I squeeze my eyes shut and hold my breath. So close I reach my arm behind me and fist his hair, needing something to hold onto.

And then his hand is gone. I gasp and grunt in frustration, my orgasm clawing its way to the surface but unable to break free. The pressure in my lower belly is almost painful with my pent-up release.

Weston just chuckles and slides his hand down my thigh, lifting my top leg and guiding it to rest over his. This way, I'm opened up for him, giving him more access.

"That's it, baby, goddamn, you need to come, don't you?"

"So bad," I respond, my voice nothing but a breathy whimper.

Weston slowly eases his finger into my entrance, just that little bit stretching me deliciously. "How are you so tight?" he grunts, sliding another inch inside me.

I clench around him, coating his hand in my juices as he starts to fingerfuck me in a steady rhythm. He grinds the palm of his hand down on my little bundle of nerves, keeping me right on the edge, the pure bliss amplified by the slight sting of being stretched. God, what's it going to feel like when he fucks me for real? The thought has me thrusting my hips forward, trying to get him deeper.

There's an intense pressure building low in my belly, throbbing outward with each steady stroke. The storm rages outside, but it's nothing compared to what's stirring deep in my core. I tighten my grip on his hair, pulling him toward me, letting him know I'm here with him and want this so, so bad.

He groans and sinks his teeth into my exposed shoulder, just enough to sting and cause a jolt of lighting to flash through my body. Or maybe the lighting is from outside. Either way, I feel it with my entire body, electrifying every inch of me, inside and out.

Weston adds a second finger, making me cry out with overwhelming pleasure. When he curls his fingers up, hitting some super sensitive spot, my entire body spasms, sending more electricity flowing through my veins.

"Weston," I moan. "Weston..."

Rain pelts against the windows, the wind nearly deafening, even from inside his apartment. I feel every muscle draw up tight as my joints lock, preparing for the onslaught of my release. Lighting illuminates the room for a brief second, the air growing still, the whole world seemingly lying in wait for my inevitable end.

Thunder tears through the sky as my orgasm tears through my body, pleasure cracking me open and vibrating through me. Another clap of thunder drowns out my screams as I pulse and thrash and claw at Weston's scalp, digging my fingers into his skin to anchor myself.

He doesn't stop, not for a second. My orgasm continues to devastate me, to the point I see black dots clouding my vision. I gasp for air, nearly coming again as oxygen fills my lungs. With a final, shuddering breath the last of my release drains from me as the rumbling thunder dies down.

"Holy shit," I barely manage to whisper as I gulp down air. I'm still trembling, my muscles feeling weak and worn out from how hard I came.

Weston groans, his fingers still buried deep inside my cunt. Slowly, so slowly, he removes them, a sudden rush of liquid pouring down my thighs. He makes some low, guttural noise, and I turn my head to look at him over my shoulder. To my absolute shock, he sucks on his digits, tasting my cream. I don't know why that turns me on so much, or how I can even be turned on so soon after coming my damn brains out, but I feel deliciously wicked and wanton.

In my blissed-out daze, I manage to roll over and push Weston on his back. He looks a little shocked and to be honest, I am too. But I'm also feeling bold and confident, which is something I haven't felt in years. I want to embrace it, however fleeting it may be.

Weston's surprised, curious expression turns dark when I place a kiss on his collarbone, his chest, and on down his torso, darting my tongue out to lick the ridges and grooves of his defined abs. I scoot down and hook my thumbs into his boxers, looking up at him when he hisses.

"What are you doing, baby?" he groans. Instead of answering with words, I pull his boxers down enough so I can grip his thick cock. "Fuck," he growls. "You don't have to do anything you don't want to." His voice is pained, but sincere. Good thing I have no intention of stopping.

"And if I do want to?"

"Shit, then I'm all yours, sunshine."

I smirk at him, his dark gaze and flaring nostrils spurring me on. I pump my fist up and down his considerable length, fascinated by the way it seems to grow and twitch in my hand. A steady stream of precum is leaking from the tip and I have a sudden intense desire to lick it off.

So, I do.

I follow my base urges, not pausing to question or doubt myself. It's such an empowering feeling, owning another person's pleasure. Weston groans loudly then curses under his breath. I take my time exploring him with my tongue, licking up and down his shaft, finding what he likes most. I've never done this before, but my inexperience doesn't slow me down.

I open my mouth and slowly sink down on his thick, rigid cock. I only manage to stuff a few inches inside, but I fist the base of his cock and stroke him roughly as I start to bob up and down.

His moans of pleasure encourage me to keep going, to take more of him. I reposition myself so I'm on my hands and knees, leaning over his side to give me better leverage. Weston threads his fingers through my hair, gripping me firmly, but gently, guiding me and setting a steady rhythm.

He trails his hand down my neck, squeezing the back of it slightly, sending a shiver down my spine. I suck on him harder, hollowing out my cheeks as I take him deeper, deeper, deeper. A muffled cry escapes my lips when Weston' fingers dip into my slit and begin rubbing my swollen bundle of nerves. I jerk and buck my hips backward, surprised I could be so close to falling over the edge again.

I'm so lost in what we're doing, it's like my body is moving on its own, his pleasure dictating my pleasure, his movements guiding my movements. I cup his balls, squeezing gently, and then more firmly when he growls.

"Fuck," he grunts, slapping my ass. "Get over here, baby. Need to taste you."

My mind is all jumbled from being on this high for so long, I'm not sure I understand what he's talking about. Weston must sense my hesitation because he grips my hips and moves my body for me. I can't focus on that, however. I'm too busy trying to fit all of his thickness into my mouth. I'm determined to make him come as hard as he made me come.

It's only when I feel his hot, wet tongue flick against my clit, do I realize what he's doing. I pop off his dick and look at him over my shoulder. He somehow got me to straddle him, my dripping pussy hovering over his lips as he licks me up and down. I'm momentarily frozen, a shiver of pleasure rocketing through me as I watch him eat me out. Weston squeezes my ass and then spreads me wide open, giving himself better access.

I turn my attention toward his cock once more, licking him up and down before kissing the very tip. Weston scrapes his teeth along my folds, sucking and nipping and making me shudder against his mouth.

I part my lips and sink down on him once more. My motions become rough and jerky as Weston devours me, sucking on my clit and then darting his tongue in and out of my entrance. I moan around his length, making Weston growl. The vibrations hit me deep in my core and radiate out, singing my nerves as I shove my face further down his cock until I choke on him. But I don't stop.

Breathing through my nose, I relax my throat and keep pressing down until the head of his dick pops into the back of my throat.

"Shay!" he cries out. The sound is muffled and broken from where he's buried between my thighs. He licks me up and down in furious strokes until my legs are shaking so bad, they almost give out. I pull back and gasp for air before sucking him down once more.

Incredibly, I feel his dick swell up even more. I want his cum on my tongue, in my throat, every-fucking-where. I've never had filthy thoughts like this, but it feels right, at least with Weston.

"Gonna come, baby. Gonna come so hard. Gotta get off..." his sentence is cut off with a savage roar, his shaft twitching, and then unleashing rope after rope of cum down my throat.

My orgasm slams into me unexpectedly, causing me to pull off his still-spasming cock. I bow my back and claw at his thighs, tipping my face toward the ceiling as I'm torn apart by my sudden, overwhelming release. I'm vaguely aware of his hot, sticky seed hitting my neck and dripping down my chest, but I can't stop shouting his name as I convulse and then collapse on top of him.

I'm panting for air as I rest my forehead on his thigh, my body too weak to move off of him. Weston is kissing my thighs so sweetly, bringing me down slowly, almost tenderly, if that's even a thing after the intense, life altering way we both fell apart.

Eventually, I roll to the side and flop down next to him, still trying to catch my breath. A shudder ripples through me and my violent heartbeat settles after a few deep breaths. Weston manages to gather my limp body up into his arms, draping me over his chest.

"God, Shay," he whispers, combing his fingers through my hair. "You're incredible."

"Mm," is about all I can say at the moment. He chuckles and places the sweetest kiss on top of my head.

Somewhere in the back of my mind, I know we probably need to clean up, especially since I have Weston's release all over my chest and neck, but I find I can't move, even if I wanted to. And I don't want to. As twisted as it is, I think...*I think I like being marked by him.*

"Fuck, I like it, too," he grunts, tightening his hold on me.

Crap, I didn't mean to say that out loud, but knowing he's just as dirty and wild with need as I am sinks down inside me. He's kind of perfect. I didn't know I wanted that in my life, but now I don't know what I'd do without it. I still don't know what's going to happen after the play, but I want to enjoy this, enjoy *him* as much as possible.

"Whatever you're thinking about, let it go, sunshine. This is real. You and me. Right here. We're real."

"So real," I whisper, nodding into his chest. He grunts in approval, making me giggle.

I let my eyes close and snuggle closer to him, sighing contentedly when he reaches out for the blankets and pulls them over us.

"Get some sleep, little sunshine," he murmurs before kissing the top of my head again. I nod and relax completely, melting into the warmth and safety of his embrace. Weston combs his fingers through my hair once more, like he can't get enough. It makes me feel beautiful and precious and seen for the first time in so long.

It's that thought that sends me off to a peaceful, all-consuming sleep.

Chapter 9

Weston

I woke up with the sun, but I've been holding Shay in my arms and watching over her for a few hours now. Creepy? Yes. Necessary for my survival? Also yes.

She's more relaxed than I've ever seen her and damn if that doesn't make me want to beat my chest and roar with pride. She trusted me with her body, her pleasure, and her safety last night, and I will never take that for granted.

Shay stirs slightly, nuzzling her face into the side of my neck and pressing herself impossibly closer into my side. I chuckle and spread my hand out over her lower back, keeping her snuggled up against me.

With my other hand, I gently comb my fingers through her soft hair, sparkling in the golden morning light. She's so damn beautiful it hurts. Every time I see her hair down, I'll be reminded of last night and the way she surrendered to my care. My touch. My tongue and lips and teeth.

Jesus, every inch of her is exquisite. Her smooth, creamy skin, perfectly perky tits, and wet, velvet heat...and her mouth. God, when her lips wrapped around me, it took every ounce of self-control I had not to fuck her face.

More than that, however, was the look she gave me right before she pulled my aching cock out of my boxers. My girl had a bold, playful, lustful look I've never seen before. Confidence lit up her features, even in the dark room. I know hardly anything about her past, but I know she hasn't given that look to anyone in a long time. Maybe ever.

"Weston?" Shay's soft, scratchy voice breaks through my thoughts. She lifts her head slightly, barely blinking her sleep-heavy eyes open.

"Morning, sunshine," I whisper, leaning down to kiss her forehead. She makes the most adorable grumpy sound and buries her face into my chest while pulling the blanket over her head. I chuckle and try to peel it back, but she grunts and hangs on even tighter.

"Wumphtymsit," she mumbles.

"What?" I ask, laughing softly while sliding down under the blankets to join her. When she doesn't respond, I find her face and tilt it up, pressing kisses on her nose and cheeks before resting my forehead on hers. The blankets form a protective shield around us, keeping the world out as we hold each other close.

"Hi," Shay murmurs, her eyes still closed.

I grin at her sweetness, even though she's clearly not a morning person.

"Hi," I reply, pressing my lips to hers in a brief kiss. I feel her lips pull into a smile beneath mine. Something about that settles deep in my bones. I like that my kisses make her smile.

Shay opens her beautiful brown eyes, looking at me for the first time this morning. "Oh!" she exclaims, throwing the blankets off and sitting up. "What time is it?"

That must have been the first question she asked. I sit up as well, looking at the clock on the nightstand. "Just past seven thirty."

"Shoot. I should check in with work and see if they lost power."

"But it's Saturday," I remind her, leaning over to kiss the side of her neck. She sighs so sweetly for me, her eyes fluttering closed.

"I...I should run errands," she says half-heartedly.

"Screw errands," I grunt, nipping at her pulse point just the way she likes.

"I-I need to check on Ainsley."

"That's what phones are for." I continue kissing up her neck and then gently pull her earlobe through my teeth.

"B-but..."

"Are you trying to find an excuse to leave, Shay?" I ask as I guide her to lie on her back. She follows my command, making me unreasonably happy. "Because I can think of a few ways to make you stay." I cage her in with a hand on either side of her head. She's absolutely otherworldly with her luminescent, white-blonde hair spread out over my pillow, a playful smirk tugging on her lips, and those bright, mischievous brown eyes shining up at me.

She shakes her head no and bites her bottom lip, making me groan in the back of my throat. "I'm not trying to leave, but I'm not opposed to exploring those ways—"

I cut her off with a forceful kiss, all too aware that we're both still naked. Shay parts her legs, making me growl as I settle between them. I rub my body up and down hers, sucking on her tongue as I feel her with every part of me. Her hard little nipples scrape up and down my chest, her soft thighs cradle my hips, and her mouth molds to mine, giving and taking in equal measure.

My rock-hard dick nestles into her dripping wet heat, just enough for her to rub herself on the underside as I thrust gently, tapping her clit with the head of my cock. Shay moans and grinds against me, her walls fluttering around me and releasing more of her arousal.

I grunt, tearing my mouth from hers so I can kiss down her neck. I scrape my teeth along her collarbone, then trail kisses over her chest until I get to her mouthwatering tits. I felt them last night, but I didn't get to see them in the darkness. In the soft morning light, however, she's on full display. And I can't wait to worship them the way they deserve.

My lips wrap around one pebbled peak and I suck, groaning when she bows her back. I slip one hand underneath her, pulling her closer to me so I can feast on her.

"Oh, Weston," she breathes out, wrapping her legs around me. I grunt, switching to her other breast while still rubbing her sensitive little button with my shaft. It'd be so easy to pull back and push my length into her tight little hole, but I won't. Not yet. Not until she's begging for me, delirious with the need to be filled.

I pick up speed, needing to feel her come with my cock gliding through her folds. Tugging her nipple through my teeth I nearly come myself when she shudders and lets out a broken cry. I repeat the same move on her other breast, making her squirm beneath me and dig her fingernails into my shoulders.

"That's it, baby. Come for me. Come all over me, Shay." My voice is deep and scratchy. Feral.

"Y-ye-yes," she stutters out, bucking her hips as she trembles and breaks apart for me. "God, Weston…"

I watch her orgasm seize her body, starting with her pussy snapping around me, then working its way outward, pushing the air out of her lungs and forcing a scream from her mouth. Seeing her face twisted up in ecstasy is my undoing.

I pull back slightly, just enough to grip my cock and pump the fucker furiously. I press the very tip to her pulsing bundle of nerves and let go, growling as I watch my cum cover her pussy. Shay bows her back and whimpers, rubbing herself against me as I keep coming in waves.

Eventually, our orgasms fade, and I find myself collapsing on top of her. I try rolling off, but Shay hooks her ankles behind my back and wraps her arms around my neck.

"Stay," she whispers.

"I don't want to hurt you."

"You're not capable of hurting me." Her response nearly brings tears to my eyes. She's right, of course, but I love that she's finally getting it. She's safe with me. "I'm safe with you," she says softly, echoing my thoughts. "I like feeling the weight of your body. It's like…"

I lift my head from where it was buried into the side of her neck, waiting for her to finish her sentence.

"What's it like?"

Her face flushes bright red, and I can't help but kiss her cheeks. She's too damn adorable for her own good.

"You feel like the biggest, warmest, comfiest blanket. Is that dumb?"

I grin at her and press a quick kiss on her lips. "It's not dumb at all. It's perfect, actually. When I first saw you, I wanted to wrap you up in a blanket and kiss you."

"You did?" She giggles, her eyes sparkling with a joy she's only recently started showing me.

"I did," I confirm, resting my forehead on hers. "Lucky me, I get to be the blanket wrapped around you," I tease.

"I think I'm the lucky one. I got the sexiest blanket ever." She smirks, making me pull her bottom lip through my teeth and kiss her soundly. I can't help it. Every single thing she does drives me crazy with need.

"I promise to be your blanket any time, sunshine. That's why you should hang out with me today. We don't have rehearsal, you don't have work, and I want to spend every second I can with you."

I was hoping my words would make her smile, but instead her brown eyes dim with sadness. Shay looks away from me, taking all of her sunshine with her. I gather her up in my arms and flip our positions so she's laying on top of me. Gently cupping the back of her neck, I guide her head up so she has to meet my gaze.

"We're not over when the play is over," I tell her, begging her with my eyes to believe my words. "I don't know what that looks like, exactly, but you have to know by now I want more than just a few weeks with you."

"How long do you want with me?" she asks tentatively.

I want to tell her *forever*, but I don't want to scare her off. "However long you'll have me," I say instead. She smiles once again, the golden sparkle returning to her eyes. I've missed it in the short moments it was gone. "How about we take it one day at a time. Starting with a date day with me."

"Date day, huh?"

"Mmhm," I respond, pulling her closer so I can kiss the tip of her nose.

"And what does one do on a date day?"

"Whatever the hell one wants."

She laughs at my response, hitting me on the chest playfully. "Fine, what will *we* do on our date day?"

I think about all the things I want to do *to her* today, but that will have to wait. I've been to Seattle a few times over the years, but the only places I know about are over-the-top fancy and ridiculous. Pricey restaurants, venues, specialty boutiques. I don't think Shay would like any of that. Not just because of her anxiety, but because that's not who she is. She's not impressed by money or status, which is more than I can say about damn near everyone else in my life.

But what else do I have to offer her? The man who stepped off the plane in Seattle seven weeks ago is almost unrecognizable from the man currently holding the most precious woman in his arms.

I've been so focused on breaking down the walls around Shay's heart and helping her see her light that I didn't realize until this moment how much she's changed me as well. I was aimless and restless long before I came here, but with Shay by my side, I know exactly who I am and what I want out of life. I want to be her protector, her biggest supporter, the one who calms her anxious thoughts. I'm hers, through and through, and my only goal now is to make her know she's mine and keep her with me forever.

"Oh! I have the best idea!" Shay exclaims, pulling me from my thoughts.

"Staying in bed naked all day?"

"Close. Getting dressed and leaving," she says with a sassy little smirk. I pout dramatically, and she laughs at me, her body shaking on top of me in the sweetest kind of torture. This woman is my whole world and her laughter is my sun. "You'll like it. I think."

"I'm sure I'll love anything, as long as we're together."

"Now I *know* that's a cheesy line from a movie," she says, quirking a cute little eyebrow up in an accusatory look.

"Nope. That cheesiness is all me, baby. Think you can handle it?"

She tries hiding her smile by nibbling on her bottom lip, but it's no use. She smiles with her whole face and I love it. "I guess we'll see."

Shay moves off of me, climbing out of bed. I reach for her hips to pull her back, but she jumps away from me, her laughter echoing around the room. I growl and hop out of bed on the other side, looping my arm around her waist when she tries to get around me. I spin her and lock my arms around her, drawing her in for a hug. I intended to kiss her until we both were out of breath, but my body must have sensed she needed this instead.

My girl leans into me, pressing her still naked body against mine. I rock her back and forth, tucking her head under my chin. I don't know how long we stay like that, but eventually we break apart.

Looking out the window, I see broken tree limbs, which reminds me there was a nasty storm last night. "Get cleaned up, sunshine. I need to make some calls about getting the power turned back on."

"Oh yeah. I kind of forgot about that. I need to call my neighbor and check in," she says, bending over to pick up her clothes. I groan at the sight of her round, juicy ass. The little minx wiggles her hips, giving me a show.

I step up behind her, gripping her hips, and grinding her against my growing erection. "Then I did my job right last night," I whisper, sliding my hands around to her front and cupping her breasts.

"Y-yeah," she says, her breath catching in her throat. "You were pretty okay."

She looks at me over her shoulder, rewarding me with another flirty, playful smirk. God, I love this woman.

Woah.

Holy shit.

I wait for the panic to set in, or for doubts to flood my mind, but instead, I feel more settled than I've ever been. Now that I have a name for these crazy feelings and obsessive thoughts, all is right in my world. Everything comes into sharp focus. I love her so damn much. It's unlike anything I've ever experienced. That one, four-letter word courses through me and sinks down deep into the very core of who I am.

"Weston? Are you alright?" Shay asks, turning around and cupping my face. She's so perfect and sweet and gorgeous.

"Yeah," I assure her. "More than alright. I was just thinking about something." I don't think she's ready to hear about my revelation. Soon, though.

"What were you thinking about?"

"I'll tell you later." I give her one last kiss, then spin her out of my arms and give her ass a light smack.

"Hey!" Shay says indignantly. Her eyes are bright and playful, letting me know she's not really upset.

"Go on, get ready for our date day, sweetheart. I'll make some calls."

"I only have my clothes from yesterday," she reminds me.

"That's fine by me. I don't care what you wear as long as—"

"I'm with you," she finishes. "You're starting to get predictable, Haze."

I growl and storm toward her, curling one arm around her waist while the other supports her back as I dip her low and hover my lips over hers. "I'll just have to try harder to impress you, then," I murmur. She opens her mouth to respond, but I swallow down her words, claiming her with all of me.

"Wow, okay, then," Shay breathes out once I tear my mouth away from hers to gulp down air. I grin and set her upright, pressing a kiss to her forehead before sending her toward the bathroom to clean up and call her friend.

***

"I know, taking you to Pike Place Market is kind of cliché, but I figured you'd be right at home."

My girl is showing me more and more of her feisty side, and while I love it, it's creating quite a problem with my dick. Namely, that the damn thing is about to bust out of my jeans.

"First I'm predictable and now I'm cliché?"

"Pretty much," she teases.

"Good thing I like you, or else I might be offended." I wink at her so she knows I'm joking.

Shay spends the next few hours showing me all the touristy things, from fish being tossed around the market to the gum wall. Then she takes me to some unexpected shops, like an entire store dedicated to selling Polish pottery and a hole in the wall that sells vintage comic books and vinyl records.

I'm thankful for the dark baseball cap and the aviators I'm wearing, which are able to conceal my identity. The last thing I want is for us to be bombarded by fans. Shay still seems a little skittish, though she's gotten more comfortable as the day goes on. I know if anyone recognized me and crowded our space, she'd probably take off running.

Everywhere we go, Shay tells me little details and personal stories attached to each place. Her tone is wistful as if she's just remembering these things for herself. I have a feeling she hasn't been here since before whatever happened that made her so skittish. I hate that it stole not only her confidence, but her memories of anything good and joyful.

Once again, my heart grows impossibly larger, knowing that she wants to share this with me. It's so much more than giving me a tour of the market and waterfront. She's showing me more of who she is, who she used to be, and who she wants to be in the future. I just need to convince her I'm in her future as well.

"Okay. I have one last place I want to show you. It's... a little unconventional, but it's worth it."

"I'll follow you—"

"To the gates of hell and back?"

I pull her close and nip the side of her neck, making her laugh. "I was going to say I'd follow you to the ends of the earth."

"That's much more original," she says sarcastically. I kiss up her neck and take her lips in mine for a kiss that's over all too quickly.

"That's what I thought," I say with a grin. She rolls her eyes but grins right back at me. Shay leads me away from the market, across the street, and down a few blocks. My interest is piqued when she turns into the entrance of a parking garage. "Are you trying to find a dark corner to have your way with me, Ms. Sullivan?"

"Is that all you think about?" Shay asks, giving me another smirk.

"That and coming up with cheesy pickup lines." This makes her laugh, which is pretty much my only goal in life at this point.

She tugs me over to the stairwell, confusing me even further as to where she's taking us. "Trust me," Shay says, as if reading my mind.

"There's an elevator right there," I point out.

"Nope." She shakes her head and pulls me along, up the first flight of stairs. There's trash and unidentifiable spills all over the cracked cement stairs, but I follow her like a lost puppy dog. Hell, that's exactly what I am when it comes to my sunshine. Three flights later, I'm huffing and puffing. Shay turns to me, hitting me with those brown eyes of hers, full of sass. It's my new favorite look. "Have two months away from Hollywood made you go soft, Haze? It's only one more flight if you think you can last that long," she teases.

"You don't have to worry about my endurance, baby," I say, spanking her sweet, tempting little backside.

"True," she concedes, a blush creeping over her cheeks.

When we make it up the final flight of stairs, I'm expecting to be at the top of the structure, but instead, we're only about halfway up. Shay leads me to the edge of the landing, where there's a railing and a little outlook.

I'm about to ask what we're doing here, but then I see it.

I take my hat and sunglasses off so I can appreciate the spectacular view of the waterfront, including the iconic Public Market sign, the Ferris wheel, and the Puget Sound stretching far beyond that. The sun is just starting to set, orange and pink hues staining the water and very tops of the buildings below.

"It's the best view in the city. Guaranteed," she whispers, almost reverently. Shay leans against the railing, looking out over the expanse in front of us. She has a sad smile on her face, which just about breaks my heart after the amazing day we had together.

"Then why are you so sad?" I ask, stepping up behind her and looping my arms around her waist.

She takes a moment to gather her thoughts before answering me. It's another thing I love about her. Shay is intentional and thoughtful when it comes to her words, which again, is unlike anyone I've been around in a long time.

"I'm not sad, I don't think. Or, maybe I am, but not about today. Not about us. I just... I've missed this."

"Missed what?" I murmur, kissing her temple before resting my chin on top of her head. I love how we fit together so perfectly.

"Watching sunsets and laughing." Shay sighs before continuing. "I guess I'm grieving, in a way," she says quietly, talking more to herself than to me at the moment. "I was lost for a little while and I'm grieving the time I could have spent enjoying moments like this."

"I'll help you make up for lost time," I promise, tightening my hold on her.

"I'd like that." Her voice is barely a whisper, but it's loud and clear to me.

"Thank you for showing me this," I say after a few quiet minutes of watching the sun sink down below the horizon.

"Thank you for letting me."

This moment is so fragile, so precious, I want to protect it and cherish it for all time. I'll carry this memory with me for the rest of our lives. The moment she gave her heart to me. I don't think she's realized it quite yet, but it's true all the same.

"Want to go home?"

She stiffens in my arms. "Oh. Yeah. Sure, I guess I should get back to—"

"My home. *Our* home."

"Ours?" She leans forward just enough to turn her head and look at me over her shoulder. I nod and kiss her, not sure how it's all going to work out, but knowing I don't ever want to spend a single night without her in my arms.

I can tell things are getting too real, too fast for her, so I lighten the mood. "I promise not to attempt to cook for you and then end up making you cook instead."

Shay gives me a little grin, which I return. "Well, when you put it that way, how could I refuse?"

"Exactly. You can't."

I'm the one pulling her down the stairs this time, anxious to spend the rest of the evening proving to her we're perfect for each other in every way.

Chapter 10

Shay

I'm a jumbled mess of emotions as Weston and I make our way back to his place. *Our* place, or so he called it. I'm not sure what to make of that statement, but I don't have the emotional capacity to figure it out at the moment with all of the other thoughts competing for my attention.

I don't know what prompted me to give Weston a tour of the most touristy place in Seattle, aside from the Space Needle, but I'm glad I did. I had no idea I'd respond the way I did—a mix of nostalgia, happy memories, a bit of anger for not living my life the last few years, and grief for the time I lost, just like I told Weston. I'm glad he was there today. Being with him was exactly what I needed as I made my way through the heavy emotions all day.

We talked, walked around, and stole kisses here and there. Weston broke up my bittersweet sadness with his heart-stopping smiles and little jokes. He was quiet when I needed a moment to reflect, he was inquisitive when I told him stories, and he silently comforted me with a gentle touch or sweet kiss. In short, he was the perfect date, and it was the perfect day.

I'm hoping it will be a perfect night, too.

Weston reads my mind once again, reaching over the console and taking my hand in his, squeezing lightly. "There's no pressure, Shay. I just want to spend time with you."

He's being so sweet, but that's not what I want from him right now. I want him to be hungry like I am. I want him to take control like he did last night and this morning. I want him to take all of me, to complete me in a way only he can.

Today felt like closure and a new beginning at the same time. I'm not stuck in the past anymore. I don't have to live in constant fear. To be able to think that at all, especially knowing Sean is out, is freeing. A weight I didn't know I was carrying lifts off my shoulders. I can stand tall for the first time in years. I can breathe deeply and let it all go.

It's not just that I know Weston will always be there for me and protect me from any potential danger, it's that I know I have the power to overcome whatever life throws my way. I've already done it.

Again, I feel confidence shining into those dark, lonely places in my soul, lighting all of me up and making me bold enough to ask for what I want. No more shying away. No more hiding. No more letting fear dictate my life. I'm in control. And right now? Right now, I want to surrender to the man who brought all of that out in me.

I guide Weston's hand to my knee, then slowly slide it up, so his fingers slip under the hem of my dress and rub against the bare skin of my inner thigh. "And if I want more?"

He makes a sound in the back of his throat, half groan, half growl, all hunger. "You'll have to be more specific, Shay." God, his deep, dark voice wraps around me and squeezes me tight, creating the most delicious pressure in my lower belly. "What do you want, exactly?"

Weston inches his hand further up my thigh until his pinky is touching my lace panties. I try to respond, but all that comes out is a breathy whimper. He growls and hooks his finger underneath the elastic, barely touching my sex.

"Do you want me to touch you here?" he purrs, pulling the thin strip of fabric to the side as I open my legs wider for him. I nod and gasp when he drags a finger through my slit, collecting the embarrassing amount of wetness as he goes. "Jesus, do you want me to lick this mess up? Suck on your clit until you come hard on my tongue?" I whimper again and shimmy my hips, trying to get him to touch my throbbing bundle of nerves. He chuckles darkly and continues to torture me, massaging me everywhere except where I need him most.

"Weston..." I moan, bucking my hips. In the back of my mind, I know we're still in Weston's car, but my body is somewhere else completely. I'm on a different plane of existence, stuck somewhere between pain and pleasure. Blood pulses and rushes through my body, making me ache with every beat of my heart.

He groans as he zips through traffic, one hand on the wheel, one hand teasing me out of my damn mind. Weston takes sweet mercy on me, circling my entrance with the tip of his blunt, calloused finger and then pushing inside.

I clench around him, tipping my head back and clawing at the seat, the console, the side of the door, trying to find something to hold on to. I curl my fingers around the edge of my seat, giving me leverage to rock my hips back and forth.

"Do you need me to fill you up? Need me to give you every inch of my hard as fuck cock?"

"Y-yes...yes, God, yes..."

I'm right there, so close I don't even care that I'm rocking into his hand. He slides another finger into my channel and grinds the heel of his palm down on my clit. My thighs start to shake as my heart thrashes around in my chest. My joints lock and my muscles tense, every single part of me bracing for release.

And then he's gone. A frustrated cry leaves my lips and my body buzzes with my impending orgasm.

I finally open my eyes, only to see that we're parked at Weston's place. The next second, my door is being ripped open. Weston unbuckles my seatbelt and pulls me out of the car, pressing me against the side before crashing his lips down on mine.

He's not gentle or sweet. He's rough, untamed...and perfect. Weston licks into my mouth, growling as he owns me with his tongue. I meet him desperate stroke for desperate stroke, fisting his shirt and pulling him closer to me. I love feeling his hard muscles press against my body, like a protective shield, even when we're together like this. A subtle reminder that he'll always protect me. I think that's part of what makes me want to let go with him.

"Shay," he growls softly, pulling air into his lungs. He wraps an arm around my waist, holding me against him. I'm so turned on, so very wet and frustrated and needy, that I'm trembling in his embrace. My knees buckle, but Weston is right there, scooping me up in his arms. "You still okay, sunshine?" he asks while carrying me to the elevator. "We don't have to—"

"We need to. *I* need to. Please don't make me wait." I know I sound desperate, but God, I've never felt such a fierce need for anyone or anything in my life.

"Love hearing you beg for me," he grunts, still cradling me in his arms. I lean up to kiss him, but the doors ding loudly and then slide open. I pout, making Weston smirk darkly. I didn't think I could possibly get any wetter, but damn, the man is making me soak my panties.

The wicked, bold, sexy side of me I've only felt around Weston takes over. He wants me to beg? I can do that.

I tilt my head up, brushing my lips against the shell of his ear as he carries me through the living room. "I need you to fill me up with your big cock. I ache for you," I whisper. Weston lets out a wild, almost painful sounding growl. "Please, Weston. Fuck me. I need it, I need..."

"Christ, woman, you're gonna be the death of me."

The next thing I know, I'm falling through the air before my back hits the soft mattress. Weston falls on top of me, pinning me down with his weight, blanketing me in his strength. His lips are on mine, picking up right where we left off in the parking lot.

He holds himself up with one hand at the side of my head, while his other hand slides down my body, cupping my breast. He squeezes lightly, groaning into my mouth. Then his hand moves lower, gripping my hip, sliding down my thigh until he reaches bare skin. Weston squeezes me there and groans again, pulling my leg to the side so he can settle between my legs.

"I need to see you naked, but I can't stop kissing these lips," he whispers, grinding his jean-covered cock against my core as he kisses me again.

I make some desperate sound in the back of my throat, then tear my mouth away from his, breathing fresh air into my burning lungs. Weston rests his forehead on mine, taking deep, ragged breaths. Knowing he's this wound up because of me is even more of a confidence booster.

I push on his chest, giving him a devious grin as he sits up. I follow him, standing right in front of the ripped, Greek god of a man. I tug at his shirt, demanding silently for him to take it off. His eyes flash with wicked intentions that match my own as he pulls his shirt off.

My hands find his chest, my fingers teasing his skin in featherlight touches. Lower, lower, lower my exploration goes, feeling the dips in his defined chest and abs. A shiver runs through his body and into mine, drawing us closer together.

I still can't believe he wants me. I'm mostly over him being a movie star, probably because that's not what he is to me. Not anymore, at least. He's so much more than his movies, his career, and yes, the tabloids that seem to have a heyday whenever he does anything noteworthy. He's more than his fame and the money I know he has in his bank account. He's...mine.

Weston tips my chin up and kisses me soundly as his fingers find the clip holding my hair in a bun. He takes it out, tangling his fingers in my hair and tugging at the strands. I let go of every thought, moaning softly when his other hand pulls the zipper down on the back of my dress. Slowly, so slowly, he peels it away, letting the fabric slide down my body.

His mouth finally leaves mine, his eyes roaming down my chest, my torso, my legs, and then reversing their path. When Weston finally meets my gaze, he gives me a gentle, reverent look. He's letting me know he wants to cherish me as much as he wants to devour me. I feel the same.

"You're so beautiful, sunshine," he murmurs, unclasping my bra and tossing it aside. Weston bends down and kisses my neck, my collarbone, and lower, licking one nipple and then the other. He kneels in front of me, blazing a trail of kisses down my torso.

I'm trembling by the time his lips reach my mound. He places a sweet kiss there then looks up at me, as if asking permission one last time. "Please," I whisper, tangling my fingers in his hair and urging him forward.

A low, guttural sound rumbles up from deep in his chest as he hooks his fingers into the waistband of my panties and pulls them down. Balancing myself on his shoulders, I step out of the last piece of clothing I have on, standing naked and unashamed before the man I love.

I gasp softly at that realization, but then I let it wash over me and sink down deep into the core of my being. I love Weston Cooper Haze. And I'm pretty sure he's half in love with me, too.

"You okay, baby?"

"More than okay," I reassure him. "But I think you need to be naked, too, for this to work."

Weston grins at me and stands up, pulling my bottom lip through his teeth. "Love that sassy mouth of yours, Shay. It might get you in trouble one of these days."

"Oh yeah?"

"Yeah. But I think you'll like your punishment."

My core clenches and releases, making more of my arousal drip down my thighs. He's right. I think I'll like whatever he does to me.

I'm unable to keep my eyes off of his hands, which are working furiously to undo his belt and pants. As soon as he pulls the zipper down, I reach out and tug his jeans and boxers down, eager, desperate, hungry for more. For everything.

Weston helps me, then grips my hips and walks me backward until my knees hit the edge of the mattress. He cups my face in his hands and brushes his nose up and down mine in the lightest touch.

"I don't know what happened in your past, sunshine, but I need you to know I'm your future. Do you trust me?"

"With all of me," I don't hesitate to answer. We share a tender moment, so many unspoken words passed back and forth with just one look. Then I feel his hard length graze against my center and just like that, I'm aching for his touch.

Weston tips his head back and groans when I grab his cock and rub the tip with my thumb, spreading his precum around. "Fuck, you feel so good. I'm clean, Shay. I haven't been with anyone in almost two years. I want inside of your tight, wet heat with nothing between us, but I'll put a condom on if you want."

I know I should tell him I've never done this before, but instead I say, "I'm on the pill. I'm clean, too." He grunts in approval. "Now get inside me right the fuck now."

"Goddamn," he growls, pushing me down on the bed.

I'm expecting him to join me, but he sinks down to his knees instead. Weston grips my thighs in his large hands and pries my legs apart. I cry out and bow my back off the bed when he presses his thumb over my clit. A sudden powerful burst of pleasure slices through me and rattles me to my core. I'm still so on edge from the drive home and the way he's been teasing me since we got here.

My pleasure grows more intense when I feel his tongue slide through my dripping wet folds, licking me and nipping at my sensitive flesh. He nudges my clit with his nose and then spears his tongue into my little hole, scooping out my juices and drinking them down.

Weston drags his tongue lower, lower, lower, until it's teasing my back entrance. I gasp at the filthiness of it all, but the forbidden nature makes me even wetter. He licks around the tight ring of muscles and growls.

"Holy fuck," I whisper. "Ohmygod, Weston, oh fuck," my whisper turning into a loud moan when the very tip of his tongue pushes inside. He rubs my clit in furious circles, and I grip the sheets, twisting them in my fists as my body expands and contracts. "I'm..."

I shatter before I even finish my sentence. My orgasm rushes through me with such intensity, I shoot up off the bed, trying to escape the overwhelming pleasure. Weston shoves me back down with a hand spread out over my stomach. He holds me there, making me feel all of it, every last drop of bliss.

He grunts in satisfaction, crawling up my body and crashing his mouth down on mine in a passionate kiss. "Needed your taste on my tongue before I fuck this tight little pussy for the first time."

Leaning back slightly, he gathers my hands and guides them over my head. Pinning my wrists down, Weston drags his thickness through my folds, coating himself in my cream before lining up with my entrance.

"Ready, sunshine?"

"So ready," I breathe out.

He kisses me as he thrusts all the way inside, tearing through the last barrier between us. I tense up at the slight pinch deep in my core, holding my breath until it passes.

"Holy shit, baby. I didn't know. I didn't know..." I open my eyes and stare into his deep, dark green irises. He looks so pained it nearly breaks my heart.

"I'm okay," I promise him. "I wanted it to be you. I want you so bad, please don't stop."

"I'm gonna make you feel so good. I'll take care of you, Shay. Always."

I nod my head and clench around his hard length, making him groan. I'm so full, stretched to the point of pain, but in the best way possible. It heightens my pleasure, sparks my nerves, and makes me thrust my hips, taking him deeper.

"Then do it, already," I practically growl at him. Weston chuckles, and I feel the vibrations with every inch of me, inside and out.

He leans down and kisses along the side of my neck, biting down gently on my pulse point. I writhe beneath him, pleasure taking over the pain. Weston pulls out almost all the way, hovering above me and driving me crazy.

Weston gives me a dark, delicious look before thrusting back inside me. His thickness scrapes along my walls, the friction like striking a match as instant, overwhelming heat engulfs me. I bow my back and push against his hand still holding my wrists, grateful for some kind of anchor in the raging storm of sensations.

He pulls my leg higher up on his hip, changing the angle. I whimper as his cock slides against some magical place inside me that has me sobbing his name louder with each thrust. Weston snaps his hips against mine, grinding his pelvis against my clit while hitting that spot over and over.

Weston grunts my name every time his balls slap against my ass. I can feel him losing control, his strokes becoming deeper, harder, so damn rough. I love it. I convulse as he thrusts into me relentlessly. The exquisite pleasure bordering on pain builds and builds, higher and higher, one more, one more, again, again...until I break. Shards of pleasure cut me and heal me as I cry out for him over and over.

My orgasm rips through me, holding my body hostage, forcing me to feel every wave of bliss until tears drip down my face and I'm a sweaty, soaking mess beneath him. Weston stays still, buried deep inside my spasming pussy.

When the last of my pleasure leaves me, Weston growls and slams into me, letting go of my wrists and sliding his hand down my body. He squeezes my breast, leaning down and bringing the nipple to his mouth and lavishing it with attention until I'm shaking beneath him.

"Oh, God, Weston," I choke out. I claw at his back as he rips me apart in the best way possible. Each gut-twisting stroke winds me up higher and higher, until I'm right on the precipice, teetering on the edge.

His hips stutter as he loses his rhythm and starts rutting into me. Weston's fingers dig into my hips as my nails bite into his skin, both of us clinging on to this tension filled pleasure. A shiver runs through me, followed by another and another until I'm shaking violently.

We both cry out as his hot seed spills into me. Wave after wave of his cum splashes into my pulsing channel and then drips out, and still, there's more. My pussy snaps around him as I sob out my climax.

I'm gasping for air as I float back down to earth, the oxygen burning my lungs and yet somehow sending jolts of pleasure to my core. Weston buries his face into the side of my neck and I wrap my arms around his torso, keeping him on top of me while we catch our breath.

"You're perfect," he whispers. "You're all mine." I nod and pull him closer until most of his weight is resting on top of me. Weston seems to understand my need almost better than I do. He surrounds me with his strength, blanketing me in his warmth. "I'm right here, sunshine. I've got you."

We stay attached as long as we can, but I start to shiver from the sweat drying on my body. Weston rolls over and drags me with him, tucking me into his side. My eyelids grow heavy and my body melts into his. I'm vaguely aware of Weston pulling the covers over us, but I'm too tired, too worn out to even look.

"Get some sleep now, sunshine. I'll be right here when you wake up."

I nod, feeling safe, warm, and completely satisfied on every level. As I drift off to sleep, I swear I hear Weston say he loves me. I want to say it back, but sleep takes me before I get a chance.

Chapter 11

Weston

I lie awake, listening to Shay's soft little snores and counting her breaths. I feel each intake of air as her lungs expand and then contract. It's calming in a way I didn't know I needed. She's here, she's really here in my arms, right where she belongs.

The sun set quite a while ago, but my Shay hasn't moved and neither have I. She pretty much passed out the moment I tucked her into my side, but I don't mind. The girl deserves to rest after what we did.

God, being with her was incredible. More than incredible. It was life altering. Soul shattering. Coming deep inside her was absolutely indescribable and yet, without a doubt, the most profound moment of my life.

And she was a virgin.

Jesus Christ, a *virgin*. I never knew I was a possessive caveman until I realized I was her first. I'll be her last, her fucking *only*. She knows it, too.

I wanted it to be you. I want you so bad, please don't stop.

My dick grows hard just thinking about her words. She trusted me with her body, her virginity, her pleasure. She begged me, and God, I'll never forget our first time together. I can't wait to be inside her again, but I know my girl has to be sore. Each thrust tore at my sanity until I lost my mind completely and fucked her so damn hard.

Shay moans softly in her sleep, then wiggles her hips, trying to get closer to me. I can't stop the deep, hungry growl rising up from my chest when she adjusts her leg and grazes my hard as fuck dick. She's still asleep, but her leg hooks around mine, her knee rubbing up against my nearly painful erection.

I reach down and wrap my hand around the back of her knee. I meant to push her leg away so I don't come all over myself like a teenager, but instead, I find myself grinding against her. I sink my teeth into my bottom lip as unbelievable pleasure rolls through me. How can I be so close to the edge from just this simple touch?

But I already know the answer. It's her. Everything about her. I'll never get enough. I know I need to stop, but she feels so damn good. Precum leaks out of me, my raging hard-on needing some kind of relief. When Shay rubs her soaking wet core up against my thigh, I groan loudly, unable to contain the sound.

Shay returns my groan with one of her own, awareness slowly creeping into her movements as she wakes up. Her nails bite into my bare chest, snapping the last thread of my control. Wrapping her long hair around my fist, I tilt her head back, growling when I see her brown eyes ablaze. My lips are on hers in the next second.

I swallow down her cries of pleasure as I devour her. Her hot little body writhes against mine, creating delicious, torturous friction. I need more. Need to feel her from the inside out. Need to consume her, taste her sweat, bite her soft skin, and drink down everything she's offering.

"Weston," she whimpers into my mouth before capturing my lips once more. I pull her on top of me so she's straddling my lap. Shay breaks our kiss, gasping for air. "Weston," she says again as she rolls her hips.

Shay's pussy lips wrap around my cock, fluttering around my length and driving me insane. I've never had this overwhelmingly primal need to claim, to possess, to own someone completely. Shay rests her forehead on mine as a shudder ripples through her lithe little body. I know she's as desperate as I am when a pained whimper escapes her mouth.

She sits up, steadying herself with both hands on my chest. I grip her hips and lift her up, positioning her dripping wet hole over the head of my cock. I hiss out a breath and squeeze my eyes shut, trying with everything in me not to come like this. Her cunt pulses, massaging my sensitive dick and making me buck my hips involuntarily and slide a few inches inside of her.

"Are you sure, baby?" I grit out, though I pray to God she doesn't stop. I'd never take what she doesn't offer, but goddamn, I'm in physical pain every single second I'm not inside of her.

Instead of answering, Shay bites her bottom lip and nods, her big brown eyes telling me everything I need to know. Slowly, so slowly, Shay sinks down on my length, her pussy stretching obscenely wide around my cock.

I drag my eyes up her body, taking in her pale skin and white-blonde hair. She's practically glowing in the moonlight streaming through the window. I watch in awe as the silver light kisses the side of her face, her breasts, her thighs. My fingers skim over everywhere the light touches, needing to feel this goddess as she brings me unimaginable pleasure.

Shay tilts her head back and claws down my chest, gasping for air once she's fully seated. I grip her hips, anchoring her to me, keeping her right here. Her core ripples around my cock, making the fucker jerk and leak more precum inside of her.

"You feel so good," I whisper, unable to find my voice as I get lost in the way our bodies are connected on every level.

I help her find her rhythm, rolling her hips and grinding her down on my swollen dick. Each movement sends sharp pangs of ecstasy shooting through my veins. I know she feels it, too, with each breathy moan that falls from her lips.

Shay's eyes snap open, locking on mine. I see the moment she recognizes her power. Her strength. Those brown eyes turn fierce, almost feral as she lifts up on her knees and drops down on me, her little hole swallowing my dick completely.

An animalistic growl rumbles through her, wracking her body as she fucks me furiously. Christ, it's all I can do to hold on. I want this for her, need this, need her to take control and understand that I'm hers. She owns me, body and soul.

I cup the back of her neck and pull her down for a kiss, tasting her sweetness as she brings both of us closer, closer, closer...

"Weston," she whispers. "Weston...Weston...fuck..." Her whimpers turn into moans, louder, louder until she's crying out my name, her voice broken as she comes all around my cock. Goddamn, she comes with her whole body, every muscle tensing and releasing as her orgasm works its way through her.

I keep her right here with me, her forehead resting on mine as she shakes and releases more of her juices. I feel her cum drip down my dick and coat my balls...and holy hell, is she coming again? Shay buries her face into the side of my neck, muffling her scream as an intense orgasm rips through her curvy little body.

Something breaks loose inside me, leaving me unhinged and wild with need. I flip Shay onto her back and rut into her throbbing pussy, grunting with each thrust. She bows her back and wraps her legs around my hips, digging her heels into my ass.

I lean down and suck on her breast, teasing one nipple and then the other, back and forth until I feel her fingernails bite into the back of my head. She pulls my hair and tilts my head up before slamming her mouth down on mine.

My greedy girl rocks into me, meeting me frantic thrust for frantic thrust. I break our kiss and inhale sharply, feeling my orgasm barrel through me. With a roar, I let go of every fucking thing and come so damn hard I feel my bones rattle.

Shay's cries carve through the night air as her channel squeezes and snaps around me, milking me and prolonging our pleasure. We're both shaking and panting as we cling to each other, riding out the last of our climax.

I collapse on top of her, gathering her limp body up in my arms. I try rolling to the side to keep from crushing her, but once again, Shay urges me to stay right where I am. I'll be her safety blanket whenever she needs it. We stay wrapped up like that for long moments, Shay taking deep breaths while I whisper how much she means to be and that she's safe right here in my arms.

Eventually, her grip on me loosens, allowing me to roll onto my back and drape her over my chest. I comb my fingers through her hair, yet another reminder of how far we've come since I first laid eyes on her. She let me see her, feel her, and build up her confidence, even though I'm still not sure what took it away in the first place.

After a few moments of silence, I begin to worry I hurt her. I mean, God, I tore into her like a beast after taking her virginity only a few hours ago.

"Sunshine?" I murmur, cupping the back of her neck and guiding her to look up at me. "Are you alright?" She nods her head, but I can't quite see the look on her face in the darkness of the room. "Need your words, baby. Did I...did I hurt you?"

"Not at all," she assures me. The pressure in my chest releases, allowing me to breathe again. "That was..." She nibbles her bottom lip, searching for something to describe what we just shared.

"Yeah, it really was," I agree, kissing her forehead and the tip of her nose. Shay sighs contentedly before curling up on my chest again.

"Tell me about you," Shay says, surprising me.

"What do you want to know?"

I feel her shrug and kiss my chest in the softest, sweetest little gesture. "It must be difficult to be in the spotlight all the time. People probably think they know you just because they watch your movies and read articles and interviews. Tell me something I wouldn't know from a Google search."

Her response makes me smile, but at the same time, my chest grows tight. Sensing the warring emotions inside me, Shay gently rubs her hand over my heart. She's right, of course. Plenty of people think they know me, or worse, don't care about knowing me as long as I give them what they want. I've become so used to playing the role of a movie star, I forgot how to just be me.

I don't know how I'm going to answer her until the words fall from my lips. "I grew up in a trailer park in South Los Angeles."

Her hand stops rubbing my chest, and for a moment I think I might have said the wrong thing. But then she turns her head and places a kiss over my heart before resuming her tender touches. "Is that why you said you've slept in worse places?"

"Hm?"

"When you stayed all night in the hallway of my apartment building, you said you've slept in worse places."

Her voice is barely above a whisper, like she doesn't want to break the little bubble we're in. I don't remember saying that, but it's not surprising that she remembered. Shay is kind and thoughtful and so damn sweet.

"Yeah," I confirm, matching her soft tone. "It was me, my mom and dad, and my two younger siblings in a two-bedroom trailer. There was never enough space or food, so I got a job in a warehouse when I was fourteen to help make ends meet and get away from that prison."

"Fourteen?"

I nod, closing my eyes as I remember Ignacio, the man who hired me and oversaw my time at the warehouse. "They knew I wasn't legal to work, but then again, neither were half of the people there. Mostly undocumented workers, though there were a few underage kids like me as well. The job paid in cash, and the higher-ups tended to look the other way when I crashed in one of the back rooms for the night. It's actually where I met my oldest friend, Rider. We both found ourselves in need of a job and a place to stay at an early age."

Shay moves her hand from my chest so she can cup the side of my face. I look down at her, my angel, my source of peace. She doesn't say anything; she just infuses more of her quiet strength directly into my soul with her gentle touch and understanding eyes.

"When I turned eighteen, Rider and I found jobs on a construction crew. It was hard, grueling, physically demanding work, but I felt accomplished at the end of the day, knowing I helped build something."

I pause to consider that. I've never had that thought about my days in construction. I don't want to go back to that job, but it sheds some light on why I've been so discontent lately. I'm not contributing to my career or even the industry as a whole. I just fit into whatever role is set in front of me and go along with it until I collect my paycheck.

"How did you get into acting?" she asks after giving me a moment to reflect.

"A Hollywood executive happened to be walking by the job site we were working on at the time. She handed me her card and said they were filming a few blocks away and needed extras for an action scene. I thought she was kidding, but when she told me how much the gig paid, I knew I had to seize the opportunity. I met my agent on that set and he gave me more work than I knew what to do with. Fast-forward fifteen years, and here I am."

"Doing a community theater play? Oh, how the mighty have fallen," she teases. I have to grin at that. I love that she's comfortable enough to give me shit. She's everything I didn't know I needed.

I lean down and nip the end of her nose, making her giggle. I pull her bottom lip through my teeth and then sweep my tongue into her mouth.

"I'm falling, alright, sunshine. Falling for you." I grin when she rolls her eyes at my cheesy line. Shay snorts out an adorable laugh, which of course, I have to taste on my lips.

When we break apart, Shay snuggles back down into my embrace. I tuck her head under my chin and stroke her back in a calming gesture.

"For real though, how did you end up here? You didn't seem too happy about it at first."

I blow out a breath and gather my thoughts. I wasn't planning on telling her all of this, at least not yet. I want to know more about her and her past, but I get the sense she needs me to open up first. I can do that for her.

"I dated this girl..." I start, not sure how to even talk about the last few years of my life.

"Teresa Marie," Shay whispers as she tenses in my arms. I squeeze her tightly and kiss the top of her head. I hate that she feels threatened by my disaster of an ex. She's got nothing to worry about.

"Teresa is your opposite in every single way." I know I said the wrong thing when Shay tries to untangle herself from me. I hold her close, unwilling to let her go. "And I couldn't be happier about that fact. You are incredible, kind, brave, and thoughtful. You're so beautiful it makes my chest ache. I long for you every minute of every day. I fucking hate whenever we're apart. You're this peaceful, grounding presence in my life, Shay. You're so pure and genuine and sassy and sweet. You're perfect."

She stills at my words, and I worry that I messed up again. But then I feel the tension drain from her muscles as she surrenders to my care once more. I pull her closer and breathe in her honied, floral scent mixed with the lingering smell of sex. It's absolutely intoxicating, but I need to focus.

"That wasn't a line, was it?" she whispers, vulnerability dripping from every word.

"That's no line, sunshine. I mean every single word." Shay nods into the side of my neck and places a kiss there, encouraging me to continue. "Like I said, Teresa is the opposite of kind, genuine, and sweet. She's as shallow as they come. Her personality is entirely dictated by her fans and her record sales. LA consumed her and she gladly let it. Our relationship was over long before we officially broke up and honestly, I didn't realize how toxic we had become until it all ended. I wish I would have broken up with her sooner. Hell, I wish we never dated in the first place."

"Why did you?" There's no judgment in her voice, only a sincere need to understand me. Fuck if I even understand me and my choices half the time.

"I..." Furrowing my brow, I consider her question. Why did I date her? "It was expected of me, I guess. Not to date Teresa, specifically, but to find someone equally as famous to be seen out in public with. It helped her record sales and my ticket sales. She was vapid and materialistic, but so was I and everyone else in LA. In a weird way, Teresa was... safe."

"Safe?" Shay turns in my arms and props herself up on my chest, tilting her head to the side as she looks at me.

"Yeah. There was no risk of getting hurt. I wasn't looking for love and neither was she. I don't think either one of us was capable of it, at least with each other. Like I said, it was a relief when we broke up. I never missed her. Just the opposite, in fact. Kind of like what you were talking about earlier this evening about being upset with yourself for not living the last few years. I was mad at myself for wasting my time with her. I was even angrier when she caused a scene at that Broadway play."

Shay scrunches her nose up and yeah, it's as adorable as always. "I heard about that."

I sigh and tuck her back into my side, unreasonably happy when she melts into my embrace. "It was a shitshow, that's for sure. She yelled, I yelled, she tried to hit me, and I stumbled into a Russian diplomat. His security saw that as a threat and before I knew it, fists were thrown."

"Bitch," Shay mutters under her breath. God, if I didn't already know I loved her, this would have done it. My girl is taking my side. It feels good to have someone believe in me, or just flat out believe me and my side of events. Her trust in me is humbling, just like always.

"Anyway. That was the last straw for my agent and PR team. After a string of other *events*, they decided my public image needed a makeover. Supporting a community theater production seemed like a good fit."

"But you weren't on board?"

"Not until I saw you walk on stage," I tell her truthfully.

"Uh-huh," she says. I can practically hear her rolling her eyes. "I'm serious."

"Me too. But now I couldn't be more thankful for my bossy PR team sending me out here. Shay, I'm done with all that drama. No pun intended." I was hoping for a laugh, but instead, she goes rigid in my arms. "For real, sunshine. No more messy relationship drama. No more reckless behavior. No more getting into trouble just to fill a void in my life. You're everything I need, Shay. You're everything."

To my surprise, Shay laughs bitterly. "My parents would disagree," she mumbles.

"What? Why?" I lean back and tip her head up so we're face to face. "What did they say? What do you mean? Are they..." I stop myself short before I ask if they're the reason she's so skittish and lost those years of her life from living in fear.

"They're not horrible or anything," she says, easing some of my anger. Though, if it wasn't her parents that caused her fear, who did? And more importantly, how can I find them and make them suffer? "I grew up with old money—the kind of money that bought a private education, lavish vacations, mansions on secluded islands, and enough staff for my parents to ignore me until they needed to marry me off to someone as part of a business deal. There was this one guy—"

"Mine," I growl, closing the distance between us and molding my lips to hers. The thought of her belonging to someone else, being pawned off by her parents, makes me livid.

"Yours," she murmurs when we break apart. Her response calms me down and when her lips brush against mine in the whisper of a kiss, I feel myself relaxing completely.

There's so much left unsaid, but Shay yawns and snuggles into me, resting her head on my chest. I pull the blankets over us and wrap my arms around her, holding her until her breathing evens out and her body goes heavy with sleep.

I want to know everything about her, but she's giving me little pieces of her past, breadcrumbs to her secret pain, her heart, and her very soul. We grew up in two completely different worlds, but we somehow found each other. I'm hit with the same feeling as when I first saw her that day up on stage. She's the most precious thing in the world and I'll do whatever it takes to protect her. I just hope she trusts me enough to let me know how to keep her safe.

Chapter 12

Shay

It's been the most incredible week with Weston. I've spent nearly every night over at his place. When we're not getting lost in pleasure and exploring each other's bodies, Weston and I talk and laugh and cook together. He's still a pretty terrible chef, but we've made progress. He can now make a mean box of mac n' cheese.

I smile at the memory of him serving us, his boyish grin and eyes shining with more than a little pride at the meal he provided for us. I like knowing I can teach him things and contribute to this relationship—if that's even what it is. We haven't talked much about it, other than when Weston said he wanted everything with me and that we're not over when the play is over.

I haven't pressed the issue, though I very much want to know what's going to happen next week after the final showing. He told me about his ex and how terribly it all ended. He also said he was done with relationship drama. The last thing I want is to scare him away by talking about houses with white picket fences and kids running under foot. Rationally, I know it's too soon to know that I want him in my life forever, but everything in me says he's the one.

Who else would be so patient with me? So kind and caring, despite what a mess I am? And let's not forget about how he worships my body as if I'm the most beautiful, precious thing in the world. *Precious.* That's exactly how he makes me feel. Not precious in the sense that I'm a fragile thing, but more like I'm his whole world and it's his job to protect me. I see it in his eyes every time he looks at me. I didn't recognize it before, but I think he's looked at me that way from the very beginning.

That's why I'm struggling to open up to him about Sean. I started to tell him about my parents and how their goal is to set me up with some rich asshole as a means to gain more wealth, but his reaction told me everything I need to know. He growled that I was his and god, I loved it. The thought of anyone else being that possessive over me sends chills down my spine, but coming from Weston, it made me feel... well, precious.

I know he'd do anything to protect me, including jeopardizing his career. If he found out about Sean and knew he was out, I know Weston would seek him out and punish him. Part of me wants that. I want Sean to feel the fear he instilled in me. I want Sean to pay for his sins and I want Weston to be the one to collect his debt.

But Weston said he's done with reckless behavior and relationship drama. Having a vengeful stalker is a recipe for both drama and recklessness. It would kill me to get Weston involved in my mess, especially when the whole point of him coming out here in the first place is to clean up his image.

Besides, I have no reason to believe Sean is out to get me. Yeah, he threatened me when he was arrested the night of the attack, but that was years ago. Maybe he's changed and received the help he so clearly needed. I have to believe that. I need to believe it for my own sanity, even if it means ignoring that tiny little voice of fear in my head and the sinking feeling in my gut. It's just my anxiety. At least, I hope it is.

I'm startled out of my thoughts when I feel arms wrap around me from behind. I gasp and try to escape, clawing at whoever is behind me.

"Woah, hey, it's just me," Weston says in a soothing voice, dropping his arms immediately and giving me space. God, thinking about Sean has me on edge, which is the last thing I need the day before opening night.

"Oh, hey." I try to sound casual as I turn around to face him.

"Are you okay, sunshine?"

"Y-yeah," I say with a shaky voice. Dammit. "I'm good. Just nerves about tomorrow, I guess." I give him my best smile, hoping to reassure him. From the concerned look on his face, I don't think I pulled it off.

Weston furrows his brow and opens his mouth to say something, but Reggie shouts his name, calling him over to help with something. He rolls his eyes and clenches his jaw, no doubt annoyed by Reggie's timing. For once, I'm thankful for the rude, portly director. I don't know if I could handle any more of Weston's kindness and worry. I might just break, but neither one of us is ready for that discussion, especially right now with the final dress rehearsal about to start.

I give Weston another smile, this time a little more genuine. He bends down and kisses my cheek, then brushes his lips against the shell of my ear. "You're safe here, sweetheart," he whispers. How does he always know exactly what I need to hear? "And you're going to do great out there. I've seen how much you've grown into the role, just like I thought you would. And Shay, you deserve the kind of love Seneca demands of Luther."

I'm too shocked to respond. Is he saying he loves me? Is he...?

Weston gives me a quick kiss on the lips, then turns around and heads toward Reggie, leaving me gaping after him. I mean, yeah, I love him, too, but I didn't expect him to feel the same way, and so shortly after we met.

It's just one more reason I can't involve him in my drama. I love him too much to see him sacrifice himself and his career over Sean. Especially when I still don't know if there's anything to even worry about.

***

"Seneca, baby, it's you and me against the world," Weston says, grinning at me from ear to ear.

"You and me, Luther," I confirm, giving him a bright smile filled with love. It's supposed to be Seneca smiling at Luther, but we both know it's me and Weston.

"It's impossible, everything we've been through, but every moment of heartbreak, every spark of joy, every tear, laugh, and sleepless night brought us right here. And there's no stronger love than this."

He kisses me as the curtains start to close on the final scene. Weston keeps kissing me even after the curtains are fully closed. He keeps kissing me as the lights dim and the stagehands begin moving props out of the way to set up for the opening scene once again. He keeps kissing me even when Reggie calls for us to come back on stage to discuss how things went.

Weston cradles my face in his hands, treating me with such care. His kiss is tender and full of promises, like he's trying to prove we'll be together long after the curtains close on the play for good.

I finally have to pull away from his addicting lips to breathe in fresh air. Weston rests his forehead on mine, still holding the sides of my face and keeping me anchored to him, to this moment. He lifts his head and presses his lips to my hairline, breathing me in. There's something about that gesture that nearly brings me to tears. I somehow sense he's drawing strength from me, though I don't understand how that's possible. I've come a long way since I've met Weston, but I don't think I hold the kind of strength someone like him would need.

However, the way he's holding me tells a different story. He really does need me as much as I need him, as impossible as that seems. I stand up a little taller, my chest filled with a sense of pride. Weston Cooper Haze is not only the most patient, kindest, sexiest man alive, but he wants me. He needs me. I'm worthy of his love and I'm important to him. I think I knew that all along, but it all hits me in this moment, behind the stage of the community theater, no less.

"Mine," he whispers before kissing my forehead and stepping back a bit. I can't help the smile that spreads across my face. Nothing else matters as long as I'm his.

"Mine," I whisper back. His green eyes sparkle as he grins and nods at me in approval.

"Weston! Shay! What the hell are you doing back there?" Reggie's booming voice interrupts our sweet moment. Weston growls and I giggle, making him smirk at me.

"I can't wait until I never have to hear his voice again," he mumbles before taking my hand and leading us out to the other side of the closed curtain.

Reggie proceeds to give us some notes on our performance, as well as further instructions for the crew and supporting roles. Weston sighs periodically and glances at me, rolling his eyes throughout Reggie's spiel. I love these playful moments when he turns into a mischievous, ornery kid. I know he didn't have much of a childhood and every single time I get to see that boyish grin of his feels like a win.

We're finally dismissed, and Weston makes his way toward me once again, drawn to me like a magnet. I don't mind. I like having him by my side always. Before he reaches me, however, Reggie strikes again.

"Weston, could you have a chat with Martin about scene two in act three? His lines are coming off a bit flat; maybe you can give him some advice."

Annoyance flashes across Weston's face, but he's able to school his features just in time for Reggie to walk across the stage. I know he'd brush it off if it were just Reggie, but when it comes to helping a fellow actor, Weston is all in. He wasn't always that way, or so he tells me, but we've talked about how much he loves giving guidance and pointers to those who ask. And I love the sense of pride he gets when someone takes his advice and totally nails the scene. It gives me hope that maybe he'll stick around here and explore that passion.

"Be right there," Weston says over his shoulder before turning toward me. "Wait for me, this won't take long. I want to take you out tonight, somewhere special to celebrate before the big day tomorrow."

I smile and nod, resisting the urge to throw my arms around him and have his lips on mine once more. It's turning into a real problem. He smirks and winks at me like he knows exactly what I was thinking.

I take a cleansing breath once Weston walks away. A few cast and crew members come up to chat with me, but I'm too drained to be much of a conversationalist. The dress rehearsal went well and I was even able to forget about Sean for a while, but now the nerves are creeping back in, both about the play and the man I've spent the last three years trying to forget.

I look around for Weston, suddenly feeling vulnerable and exposed. He's still talking with Martin, though he turns to look at me as if sensing my eyes on him. I give him a smile, which he easily returns before answering a question from Martin.

Deciding I need some fresh air while I wait for Weston to finish up, I head to the back exit, pushing the door open and squinting against the sunlight. Leaning against the wall, I close my eyes and take a deep breath, followed by several more.

My eyes snap open when I hear a shuffling noise at the end of the alley. I turn my head in that direction, but I don't see anything.

It's fine. It's a busy sidewalk; it could be anything, I tell myself while taking measured breaths.

Something moves in the shadows behind the dumpster, making my heart race out of control as beads of sweat form on my brow and upper lip. I ball my hands into fists, inching toward the door to the theater. I know I'm being ridiculous, and I hate that I was feeling so confident earlier in the day only to have that ripped away by nothing more than weird noises in the alley behind the theater.

When I'm close enough to the door, I spin around and grab the handle, fully intending on running inside and leaping into Weston's arms, despite how silly and irrational my fear is. Just as I'm turning the handle, I feel fingers wrap around my neck and pull me backward. I try to scream, but a large hand covers my mouth, muffling the noise.

"Thought I'd forget you belong to me?"

The rough, sinister voice crawls down my spine and scrapes along my nerves, making me twitch in Sean's grasp. His voice is repulsive and his touch makes me sick to my stomach. Sean spins me around so we're face to face. Flashbacks of that night years ago flood my mind, making it hard to breathe.

He grabbed me then, too. He shoved me into the brick wall, just like he's doing now. My head smacks against the side of the building, jarring more memories that I tried so hard to bury. Those eyes. Black, beady, sinister, and full of vile intentions. His nostrils flare, smelling my fear, and feeding off my helplessness.

I'm frozen in place, my body completely rigid, my mind stuck halfway between the nightmare of three years ago and the shock of reliving it right now. Only this time, Ainsley isn't here to save me. Weston isn't here to protect me. That just leaves me with... me.

The deranged man sneers at me, his features twisting up in a sick, amused smile. He likes seeing me suffer. He gets off on the panic he instills in the deepest part of me. That's what he's wanted all along.

"No need to be shy, little girl. You'll be mine soon enough. We'll share everything. Every. Damn. Thing." Sean punctuates each word by tightening his hold on my neck until I'm coughing and sputtering for air.

Mine.

But I'm not his. I'm my own person and I get to decide who I belong to, if anyone. I choose myself. I choose Weston. I choose the life Weston has shown me, the confidence he's built up, the strength he's given me with every look, every touch, every kiss. He's fought for me, for us, and now it's my turn to fight for myself.

A surge of adrenaline courses through my veins and I don't have time to think about what I'm doing until I'm already doing it. I stomp on Sean's foot in my four-inch heels that I never took off from dress rehearsal. At the same time, I tilt my head and smash it against Sean's nose, hoping I did some damage.

He roars out a string of curse words and releases his hold on me, stumbling backward. I could run. I could go back inside. I probably should, but I'm not done showing him he can't mess with me anymore.

I gasp for air and regain some of my senses, just in time to see Sean try to sit up. I tackle him back down to the ground and rip off one of my shoes, lifting it above my head and striking him with the long stiletto heel. He cries out in pain, giving me a sense of dark, twisted pleasure.

Something snaps deep inside. Fuck this guy. Fuck the power he's held over me for too damn long. Fuck the fear, the helplessness, the years he stole. I strike him over and over, each blow loosening the shackles of terror he's kept me in for years.

I only stop when I feel warm, familiar hands on my shoulders. Weston's touch calms me, brings me back from the edge, and quiets the rage I was lost in. I don't realize I'm sobbing and screaming until Weston pulls me off of Sean and wraps his arms around me. I'm trembling almost violently in his embrace, tears streaming down my face as I whimper with each ragged breath.

"I've got you," he whispers, squeezing me tighter like he's trying to hold me together even as I fall apart. "It's over, Shay, it's over now."

I'm vaguely aware of people moving around us, their voices fading into the background as I bury myself further into his chest. I cling to him right as my legs give out. Weston scoops me up and carries me inside, setting me down gently in one of the chairs backstage. He takes his jacket off and wraps it around my shoulders, somehow knowing that I'm suddenly freezing cold.

He kneels in front of me, cupping my cheeks and wiping away the steady stream of tears that I can't seem to control. "You're safe now, sunshine. Stay right here. I need to call the cops and then you'll tell me everything."

I want to protest, to tell him it's over like he said earlier, but one look in his deep green eyes and I know I have to tell him everything. He looks equal parts crushed and guilty, and I realize how much I've hurt him by keeping my past a secret.

I nod and let him kiss my forehead, soaking in his earthy, spicy scent, letting it surround me and bring me the familiar comfort I've only ever felt around him. Weston gives me one last look, begging me to stay here and wait for him. I nod again, silently letting him know I'm not going anywhere.

Chapter 13

Once Shay is safely inside, I allow the rage I'd barely kept at bay to take over. I throw the back door open so hard it slams against the brick wall, the deafening, violent sound matching my mood. One look at the fucker who dared to touch Shay is all it takes to tip me over the edge.

I grab him by his shirt and rip his bloody body off the ground, jarring him out of his stupor. I'm damn proud of my sunshine for kicking his ass. Now it's my turn.

The first blow knocks out a tooth, making me grunt in satisfaction. The second punch to his gut sends him right back down to the ground, sputtering and wheezing out a cough when his back hits the pavement.

The coward tries crawling away from me, but I'm far from done. I rest my foot on his chest, pinning him down as I sneer at him and spit on his face. He opens his eyes, black, disgusting little things, and then opens his mouth to say something. I don't want his words, however. I want his cries of pain as I teach him a lesson about harming my woman.

I growl at the man, killing the protest before it leaves his mouth. I watch in satisfaction as his gaze turns from defiant to defeated. And then I kick him in his side. I'm about to go at it again, but hands are grabbing me and pulling me back.

"Weston," someone says, their voice filtering through the fog of anger. "Weston, he's out cold. The cops are here."

I shake away my restraints, but step away from the man currently bruised, broken, and crumpled on the ground like the pathetic piece of trash he is. Four people step back, making me realize it took all of them to finally pull me away.

I'm shaking and panting for air as I come back down from the rage induced adrenaline high. A rough growl escapes my lips on each exhale. Jesus, I've never been this worked up before, even when I had knock-down, drag-out brawls in the trailer park. Then again, I've never had something so important to protect. Not that she needed me. My brave warrior of a woman took down her attacker all on her own and I couldn't be prouder of her.

"Ah, um, Weston, er, Mr. Haze," another voice says, bringing me back into the present. My breath is a little more even, but I'm sure I still look like a hulked-out mess. "I'm Officer Daniels, and this is my partner, Officer Menendez."

I nod in their direction, inhaling deeply to calm myself down. I know I need to give a statement and then Shay will need to give hers. I can't have her seeing me like this. She needs me to be grounded, and right now I feel unstable, and still ready for a fight at the drop of a hat.

The two officers lead me further away from the unconscious man, allowing the paramedics and another set of officers to tend to his wounds and hopefully cuff the fucker and send him away for good. I tell them about hearing a guttural, feral scream and then rushing outside, only to find the most horrific scene unfolding in front of me.

Shay was trembling and shouting and defending herself against the much larger man, holding her own, yet absolutely terrified the whole time. I have to close my eyes against the memory, reminding myself that she's safe now, and that I'll never be apart from her from this day forward.

After they get the information they need, I show them inside so they can talk to Shay. She's sitting right where I left her, though it looks like she was tended to by a paramedic while I was giving my statement. Shay has a blanket wrapped around her shoulders and a glass of water in her trembling hand. One of the stagehands is pressing a cool washcloth on the back of Shay's neck, offering silent support. I nod my thanks to the woman who stayed with Shay before I take her place.

Shay doesn't acknowledge me at first, her eyes fixed straight ahead as she shivers uncontrollably, no doubt in shock. I take the glass of water from her hand, then barely graze her forearm with the tips of my fingers. She jerks in the seat, then turns her head, her eyes meeting mine. Awareness takes over her features as tears well up in her golden-brown eyes and begin streaming down her face.

I wrap my arms around her and pull her into my side, covering her with my body as she unravels in my embrace. Shay buries her face into the side of my neck and fists my shirt, trying to disappear into me completely. We stay like that for long moments, both of us giving and taking comfort in the fact that we're here, we're safe, and we have each other.

Eventually, she loosens her grip and sits up a little straighter, though I keep an arm wrapped around her shoulders, holding her close.

"Ms. Sullivan, we're here to take your statement if you're prepared to give it," Officer Menendez says, her voice soft and gentle.

Shay looks over at me, such pain swimming in her eyes. I hold her gaze for a moment, then press a tender kiss to her temple, breathing in her sweet, floral scent. It surrounds me and siphons out the last of my fear and rage. "I'm with you every step of the way, sunshine. I'll be whatever you need."

She closes her eyes and nods her head, snuggling deeper into my side as if to borrow my strength. I'll give it all to her.

"Let's start with a few questions, if that's okay," the officer says. "Do you know the man who attacked you?"

Shay nods her head and I grit my teeth, my chest growing tight. This is who shattered my Shay's bright spirit and tried to take her light away.

"H-he... my parents..." she stutters out on a shaky breath. Shay looks over at me once again and I tighten my hold on her, letting her know there's nothing she can say that would make me leave her side. My brave girl takes a cleansing breath and pushes through her fear. Another wave of pride rolls through me as I watch her straighten her back and gain some of her confidence back. "My parents set me up with him three and a half years ago," she says, her voice steady as she speaks her truth.

"What's his name?"

"Sean McCallister. His family owns McCallister and Sons, a prominent law firm over on Bainbridge Island. My parents were hoping for an alliance, I guess. Anyway, it doesn't matter. We didn't hit it off, to say the least, but they kept inviting his family over for dinner, keeping up the pretense of us courting or something."

Shay shrugs as if that was a normal thing. Hell, from what she told me of her family, it probably was. Guilt sinks heavy in my stomach as I remember what she told me about them. Was she trying to tell me more about this Sean motherfucker? I cut her off that night, the possessive beast I didn't know I had rearing its head and claiming her, needing her to know she's mine.

"Do you have any idea what made him resurface after all this time?"

"Yeah. He, uh... he didn't handle the rejection very well when I told him we weren't together and that I'd never be with him. It was during my freshman year of college. He started showing up to my classes, hanging around my apartment, and bothering my best friend, Ainsley, if he couldn't find me. Then I started getting calls late at night and notes on my car or slipped under the front door. I didn't respond to him and after a few months, he eventually stopped. Or so I thought."

Shay takes a deep breath while the officer scribbles down notes. My heart hurts for my beautiful girl. No wonder she was so skittish. She had a stalker. One who was clearly deranged. I wish I had known. I wish she had told me. I wish she had trusted me with her past. But it's not about that right now.

"Did something else happen? These things often escalate," the officer gently prods.

Shay nods her head and sinks back into my side. I kiss the top of her head and remind her that I'm here and she's safe. "He attacked me one night when I was walking home from class," she whispers. It takes everything in me not to storm back outside and rip the bastard from the back of the ambulance and beat him all over again. "It was... it didn't end as well as this time. It could have been so much worse, though. Ainsley heard the struggle and came out with a can of pepper spray."

I'll have to remember to buy Ainsley a new car. A house. A castle. She can have whatever she wants for being there for my sunshine.

"I know it's difficult, but can you tell me what happened?"

Shay sighs deeply before answering. "He tried..." She shivers and swallows down tears. "He was going to r-ra..." Shay lets out a quiet sob, shuddering again and shaking her head. She can't say the word. Honestly, I don't think I can hear it. Officer Menendez gets the picture and jots it down in her notes. Shay gets herself together a little bit, clearing her throat before continuing. "When all was said and done, I was in the hospital for a week with a broken arm, a shattered femur, two broken ribs, and a concussion."

"Jesus," I mutter, unable to keep quiet. Shay squeezes my hand and kisses the side of my neck. How is she so fucking sweet after all of this? How is *she* the one calming *me* down?

"Sean was arrested," Shay goes on to say. "He was supposed to be in for five years, but..." she trails off and looks up at me, her eyes a mixture of sadness and regret, almost like she's apologizing. What could she possibly have to apologize to me for? "But he got out early. I received a call from the Washington State Penitentiary a few weeks ago."

"Oh, Shay," I whisper, absolutely heartbroken. That must have been the call that sent her into a panic attack the night of our date. Her eyes shimmer with unshed tears. I see so many emotions welling up inside of her. I know she regrets keeping her secret. I regret it, too, but I'm just glad it's all out in the open now. I kiss her forehead and encourage her to continue.

"Before they arrested him, he said... he said I'd always be his," she finishes, her voice barely above a whisper. I can't help the growl rumbling up from my chest, but I try to suppress it as much as possible.

"Thank you for your statement, Ms. Sullivan. Rest assured Mr. McCallister will be behind bars for a very long time. We take repeat offenders seriously and your statement all but seals his sentence."

Shay answers a few more questions about what went down today in the alley, then thanks the officers before collapsing against my chest. After one of the other actors hands me her purse and jacket from the dressing room, I lift her up into my arms and carry her out to my car, buckling her in and tucking the blanket around her.

We don't say anything on the drive to my place, both of us lost in thought and worn out from the events of the day. Once we're parked in the underground garage, I gather my sunshine up again, knowing she's too exhausted to do anything other than let me take care of her. I'm damn glad she trusts me in her vulnerable state.

I carry her into the elevator, through my penthouse, and into the bathroom. Setting her down gently on the counter next to the sink, I make sure she's steady enough to sit on her own before leaving her briefly to run a bath for her.

Silently, I strip off her clothes, piece by piece, until she's naked before me. I reach out and tuck some of her loose hair behind her ear and cup her face, drawing her gaze up toward me. I can't find the words to tell her how relieved I am, how scared I was, how precious she is to me, but I know she feels it when she closes her eyes and leans into my touch.

I guide her to the bath and help her get in before taking my own clothes off and joining her. I need to touch her, to feel her skin on mine, to hold her and protect her, and have her as close as possible as we wash away everything that happened today.

Grabbing a washcloth, I dip it into the water and fill it with the lavender scented soap I bought just for her. Gently, so fucking gently, I begin to clean my sunshine's skin, wiping away the dirt and grime and fear in tender strokes. She relaxes at my touch, releasing the tension in her muscles little by little. She lets me take her hair down and wash it as well, her shoulders shaking as she cries and surrenders to me.

When I'm done, I wrap my arms around her and guide her to lean against me. She melts into my body, the last bit of energy draining from her.

"Why didn't you tell me about Sean?" I whisper. I didn't mean for the words to come out of my mouth. I wasn't planning on having this conversation just yet, but now that my question is out there, I need to know.

She takes a deep breath and blows it out, gathering her thoughts. "I didn't want it to ruin what we had," she whispers.

"What we *have*," I correct. "I'm not leaving you, Shay. And you couldn't ruin us. Nothing you say or do could make me love you any less."

She gasps, and I realize what I said. Again, I didn't mean to tell her that right now, but I don't regret it. "Love?" she asks in disbelief.

"Love," I confirm. "I love you with every damn thing in me. It's fierce and primal, the love I have for you, but I'd never hurt you. All I've ever wanted—no, *needed*—is to protect you. I'm sorry I failed you, sunshine. I..." My voice catches in my throat as tears sting the back of my eyes. I don't let them fall, though. I need to be strong for her right now. "I love you," I repeat so we both hear it, know it, and feel it together.

"After you told me about your ex and not wanting more drama, or to act recklessly anymore, I worried about how you would react to learning about Sean."

"No drama?" I ask, confused. "Reckless?"

"Yeah. You said you were done with all of that."

More guilt pierces my chest and sinks into the pit of my stomach. Anger sits there as well. Anger at myself and my careless words, even if I didn't know it at the time. "Look at me, sunshine," I murmur, sitting her up a bit so she can meet my gaze. "Knowing about you, learning about your past, your heartaches, your dreams… all of that, it's not drama. It's me discovering how I can love you better. How I can support you and help you realize your own strength." She tries to shake her head no, but I hold her gaze steady and nod my head, begging her to listen and believe me. "As for reckless behavior, what exactly do you mean? What were you afraid of?"

"I knew you would protect me by any means necessary."

"Damn right I would," I growl softly, possessiveness creeping into my words.

"Even if it meant throwing your career away to seek justice. You already said you're on thin ice with just about everyone in your life because of some reckless choices you've made. It would kill me to know you sacrificed the one thing you've worked so hard for."

Her words absolutely wreck me. Is that what she's thought this whole time? That my career is more important than her?

"Shay, sweetheart, I don't even know where to begin." I close my eyes and breathe in deep, allowing myself to feel Shay's body against mine and smell her sweet jasmine scent. "Keeping you safe isn't reckless, no matter how I go about it. You've given my life meaning and protecting you is now my sole purpose. As for working hard… sunshine, *you* are the hardest thing I've worked for. I'd sacrifice anything for you. Everything. All I have is already yours, all you have to do is let me love you."

"Weston…" Her voice is barely above a whisper. "You really mean that." It's not a question so much as a statement for herself. I let her see all of my emotions and intentions shining through my eyes. I hope she knows I've never meant anything more. "I love you, too."

My heart stops in my chest as more tears clog my throat. "Say it again," I murmur.

"I love you."

I close my eyes and let her words wash over me. "Again."

Shay turns in my arms, pressing her lips against mine in the lightest whisper of a kiss. "I love you, I love you, I love you."

I rest my forehead on hers, unable to hold back my tears any longer. We cry together and hold each other, breaking and healing and breathing in this moment. We stay like that until the water turns cold.

After drying us both off, I dress Shay in one of my T-shirts and tuck her into bed. We still have a lot to discuss and clearly, I need to do a better job of addressing her doubts, but we're both exhausted. Shay snuggles into the blankets and gives me the sweetest, sleepiest little smile. My heart surges in my chest, knowing she can still look at me like that after everything we've been through today. I lean down and kiss the tip of her nose, smiling to myself when she giggles softly.

"I'll join you in a minute. I have a few calls to make." Shay nods her head, her eyes already half closed.

Right on cue, my phone rings. I don't even have to look at the screen to know it's Linda.

"You put a man in the hospital," she says bluntly, cutting right to the chase. I have no idea how she knows that already, but then again, I guess I pay her to always be ahead of the curve.

"And I'd do it again in a heartbeat."

"What the actual fuck, Weston?"

My eyebrows shoot up to my hairline. Linda has been upset with me pretty much since the day I hired her, but she's never let her cold, professional demeanor slip like this.

"Let him talk," I hear Ted say somewhere in the background. I must be on speaker.

"Is Matthew there, too?" I mutter.

"Present and accounted for," he confirms in the diplomatic way I've come to expect from him.

"So, out with it. How the hell are we going to spin this one, Weston?" Linda presses on, ignoring the two men with her.

"Spin it however you want, I don't care. I'll never apologize for defending the woman I love," I practically growl. There's silence on the other end of the line, so I continue. "In fact, I'm not sure if I'll need your services anymore. I don't think I'll be returning to LA, at least not in the same capacity." I'm not sure where these words are coming from, but each one fills me with more and more confidence. Of course, I'm staying here with Shay. Why would I try to convince myself, let alone anyone else, otherwise?

"Now, let's not be hasty, Weston," Matthew says.

"Let him talk," Ted grunts. I have to smile at that. I will miss the old man. He's been my only family for the last fifteen years.

"I don't have a plan yet; I just know I can't leave here. I can't leave Shay."

"Shay Sullivan?" Linda asks, her voice sounding a little perkier.

"Yes."

"Your costar?"

"Yes..." I confirm, albeit suspiciously.

"Oh. Well then. I can work with that. You fell for your costar and saved her from... something. What was it? Why did you beat the man? It doesn't matter. This is gold. It's perfec—"

"You're fired," I growl.

"No, I'm not. I'm trying to save your caree—"

"You. Are. Fired. Shay isn't a pawn. I won't allow her to be used to make me look better. I stand by my actions and I'd do it all over again to anyone who harms or manipulates my woman, physically, emotionally, or otherwise." I let the implication hang in the air. Of course, I'd never actually beat anyone in that room, but I'd damn well fire every single one of them and make sure they never find work again.

"I think he's said his piece, Linda," Ted says, taking control of the conversation. "And you've said yours. It's been a long day for everyone. Let's pick up this conversation at a later time."

Linda mutters something, followed by the sound of a chair scraping across the floor, and then a door slamming.

"I better take my leave, too," Matthew says, following suit.

After a moment of heavy silence, Ted clears his throat. "Are you doing okay, kid?"

I smile at his words. Ted has always been more of a father figure than an agent and right now, I couldn't be more grateful.

"I'm hanging in there. Better now that Sean is broken and will be behind bars soon."

More silence. I can just see him leaning back in his chair and resting his hands over his rounded belly. "You love the girl, huh?"

"Yes," I don't hesitate to answer.

"I'll be damned. You sound good. Well, you sound like shit, but you've got a purpose now, don't you?"

"Absolutely."

"No more filling the void with parties and escapades and expensive trinkets?"

"I don't need any of that anymore."

"Good, good. Glad to hear it." There's another heavy pause and then, "I'm proud of you, Weston."

I can't quite say what his words do to me. "I'll miss you, old man," I finally say, swallowing back tears for what feels like the thousandth time today. I didn't have to say it, but we both know I'm not coming back to Hollywood as an actor.

"You're not getting rid of me that easily," he chuckles. "No, I'm afraid you're stuck with me, whether I'm on your payroll or not. I can't wait to meet the little lady who broke down your walls. Good thing I don't have to. I'll see you both at opening night tomorrow, yeah?"

"I don't know if she'll be up for the play. I don't know if *I'll* be up for the play," I answer honestly.

"Well, I'll be there either way. It's your life, Weston. For the first time in a long time, I feel good about you calling the shots."

We say our goodbyes and hang up, though his words still echo in my head. It *is* my life, and I *do* get to call the shots. Right now, I want nothing more than to be with my sunshine.

Walking back to my room, I see her all snuggled up in the blankets, right where I left her. I crawl into bed behind her and curl myself around her small frame, pulling her against me. She sighs so sweetly and lets me hold her until we both drift off to sleep.

Chapter 14

Shay

"You'll never get away from me, little doll. I'll always find you," Sean spits the words in my face as he grabs my neck.

I whimper pathetically, the fight completely drained from me. He sneers, knowing he made me weak, knowing he owns me. Panic swims in my veins, making it hard to breathe.

Not again. How did he find me? How did he get out of jail so quickly? I don't have time to contemplate the answers as he lifts me up off the ground by my neck and then tosses me aside, a sinister laugh pouring from his lips and crawling down my spine as he looks down at me.

I curl into a tight ball and prepare myself for more of his wrath.

"Get up!" he demands. I can't move, let alone stand, fear paralyzing me with each breath. "GET UP!" Sean screams, becoming totally unhinged.

"No, please," I whisper, begging him to stop. "Please let me go. Please..."

"Shay, wake up." Another voice breaks through my fear, this one soothing and familiar. "It's just a dream, baby. Just a bad dream."

I know that voice, but it sounds far away, like I'm underwater and the whole world is muted. Slowly, I rise to the surface, the calming voice breaking through the terror flooding my mind. I feel a warmth surround me and then soft lips press against my forehead.

"You're safe, Shay. I've got you," the voice murmurs.

My eyelids flutter open, the last of my fear subsiding as I leave the nightmare behind. "Weston," I whisper, my voice broken and scratchy.

"I'm right here. You're safe," he says again, knowing I need to hear it over and over to believe it. He sits up and lifts me onto his lap, cradling me in his arms. I curl up into his chest, burying my face into the side of his neck. Weston's cedar and spice scent fills my lungs and anchors me to him as I surrender to his strength and comfort.

"I'm sorry," I squeak out, clinging to him like my life depends on it. In this moment, I truly feel like it does.

"There's nothing to be sorry for, love," he murmurs in the softest, most understanding voice.

We stay wrapped up in each other's arms for long moments until my shaking subsides and my breathing somewhat returns to normal. The whole time Weston whispers that he's here, I'm safe, and he loves me.

I lean back and look into the eyes of the man I love. I see so many emotions flicker across his face, the prominent one being guilt. What does he have to feel guilty about? The pain I see in his gaze tears at my heart. I lean up and brush my lips against his, needing to somehow comfort him the way he's comforting me.

"What's wrong?" I ask, resting my forehead on his.

He doesn't answer yet, he just closes his eyes and breathes deeply, tightening his hold on me.

"I failed you," he finally answers. "I failed to protect you and now you're having nightmares. I'm so sorry, Shay."

"What? No, Weston, it's not your fault."

"I should have known. I should have asked you more about your past. I should have listened when you tried to tell me. I should have—"

I cut him off with another kiss, this one deeper and filled with meaning. I know nothing I say will ease his misplaced guilt, but maybe I can show him that I don't blame him in the least. Maybe I can prove to him with my body that he's everything I've wanted and needed in my life.

He parts his lips for me, letting me slide my tongue inside his mouth and taste him. God, I missed his flavor, which is crazy since it's only been a handful of hours since we last kissed. But this is different. There are no secrets between us, nothing I'm trying to hide. He's seen me, all of me, and he loves me.

I moan softly into his mouth, making Weston growl and slide his hands underneath the oversized shirt I'm wearing. My skin prickles with awareness everywhere he touches me. I adjust myself so I'm straddling him, never breaking our kiss, our connection.

I can't help the needy whimper that falls from my lips when my bare pussy rubs up against his cock, covered only in boxer briefs. I feel him lengthen and harden beneath me, the sensation making me so, *so* wet.

Wrapping my arms around his neck, I hold him close as I grind down on his lap. Weston groans and breaks our kiss, only to nibble down my neck. I shiver and squeeze my thighs around his hips, needing more.

Weston leans back and cups my face, resting his forehead on mine. We're both breathing heavily, the air thick with what we both crave. He slides his hands down my neck, my shoulders, my torso until he grips the hem of my shirt and gently lifts it off my body.

I'm bare before him in more ways than one. I feel vulnerable and yet somehow bold. Exposed, yet covered in the safety that is my Weston. My home. My love. His fingertips trail up my sides in featherlight touches as he looks at me with a mix of awe and reverence.

Leaning forward, Weston captures my nipple in his mouth, gently sucking as his hands slide around to my back, pressing me closer to him. I tip my head back and rock my hips against his, savoring every swipe of his tongue and stroke of his fingers.

Weston hums in approval as he switches breasts, lavishing the other one with the same attention. I feel the vibrations deep down in my core, making more of my arousal drip down and coat the thin layer of fabric covering his throbbing dick. I feel it swell up even more as a soft growl rumbles up from his chest.

I slide my hands down his sculpted chest, pushing him back ever so much. He grunts in frustration like I took away his favorite toy. It makes me giggle, knowing he wants me that much.

Weston looks up at me with the softest, sweetest smile, making me melt for him, even while I'm so turned on, I'm ready to burst.

"Love that sound, sunshine. Love every single time I can get you to laugh."

God, how is this man so freaking perfect? I don't know how to respond to him with words, so I kiss him once again as my hands trail lower, lower, lower, until my fingers graze the waistband of his boxer briefs.

He tilts his head back, breaking our kiss to growl softly. I scoot back just enough to reach inside and pull him out, stroking him and rubbing his precum up and down his thickness.

"Jesus," he grunts, his muscles tensing and flexing as I pick up my pace. Weston grips my hips and lifts me up, positioning me so the head of his cock is right at my entrance. My core clenches up and releases more of my wetness, helping him to slide in easily. "This what you need, baby? Need me to fill you up?"

"Yes...God, Weston..." I breathe out, moaning as my tight channel stretches to accommodate him. I feel every vein and ridge of his shaft as he enters me. It feels so damn good to be connected like this, to be completed in a way only Weston can provide.

My hands move on their own, tangling in my hair as I stretch my body out for his pleasure. He groans and sucks on my neck as his hands slide up my back and grip my shoulders. He presses my body down on his as he grinds his thick cock against me, hitting my clit just right.

I jerk and tremble in his embrace, gasping for air when he pushes me right to the edge. Weston trails his fingers back down my spine, gripping my ass and spreading my cheeks apart as he starts to fuck up into my pulsing cunt.

"Love feeling you, Shay. Love your sexy fucking body," he murmurs, nipping at my earlobe and causing me to shudder in his arms.

"Mmhm," is all I can manage to say, too lost in the sensation of his cock scraping along my walls and hitting every pleasure point inside of me.

I feel my orgasm blooming deep in my core, throbbing outward and seizing my muscles. My joints lock up and I suck in a breath, bracing myself for what's to come. I squeeze my core around him and roll my hips in jerky motions, needing to come so bad it hurts.

Weston senses my urgency, cupping the back of my neck and drawing me down for a heated kiss. He pulls my bottom lip through his teeth before diving in, tangling his tongue with mine as he bounces me off his length. He tilts his hips and hits that one spot that drives me crazy. Over and over he hammers into me until the coil snaps and I cry out my orgasm. Pure pleasure slams into me, overwhelming my senses as I writhe and whimper and get completely swept away by my release.

When I open my eyes, I'm lying on my back, Weston hovering over me and staring at me with a hunger so fierce it makes my pussy contract again, despite just having an intense orgasm. He growls and begins moving again, his dick still buried deep inside me.

He builds us both up with slow, measured rolls of his hips. His need is palpable, but he's being so gentle with me, sliding in and out, again and again, never breaking eye contact.

Weston cups my face with one hand, wiping away a tear I didn't know was there. He kisses the spot before burying his face into the side of my neck.

"I love you," he murmurs, nuzzling into me as we make love. That's exactly what this is. It's intense, but in a different way than we've been together previously. Everything is heightened, our bodies tangling together as much as our souls.

"Weston," I whisper. "I love you so much."

His dick twitches at my words, making me moan. I love that he's as turned on by my words as he is my body. I'll never get enough of this man.

He slides one hand between my back and the mattress, pressing me closer to him, needing as much of me as possible. His touch leaves a trail of fire and awareness as he grazes his fingertips over my ass and then grips my thigh. Weston spreads me open even wider and hooks his hand behind my knee, lifting it up and changing the angle.

I gasp and whimper as he hits me so damn deep. My nails dig into his biceps as he slowly pulls out and pushes back in, going deeper with every thrust. Each time he reaches the end of me, I jerk and spasm, electricity flowing through my veins and sparking a fire deep in my core. Flames lick at my nerves as my moans turn into cries of pleasure, torture, bliss, and an almost painful need for release.

"That's it," he grunts, his hips stuttering as he picks up his pace. "Fuck, I feel you, baby. Are you going to come for me?"

I nod and whimper, my body trembling as I take everything he's giving me. Liquid heat erupts from my core, spilling out of me, making me convulse in his arms as I come. *Hard.*

Weston grunts and snaps his hips against mine, fucking me roughly as I fall apart. I can't *breathe*, he's so deep, so thick, and feels so mind-numbingly incredible. I thought my pleasure peaked, but I spasm around him again when he unleashes his cum inside me. He grunts out his orgasm, grinding his dick down as it swells up and jerks, coating my pussy with his release.

His lips find mine and he thrusts his tongue inside my mouth, swallowing down my moans and sucking the air out of my lungs. He breaks the kiss, only to scrape his teeth down the side of my neck, across my collarbone, over my breast, and down my torso.

"Wh-what are you...?"

My question is cut off when he settles between my thighs and licks my pussy. I gasp and moan loudly, my body moving on its own to grind against his face. My pussy feels raw and so damn sensitive from the orgasms I've already had, and yet each stroke of his tongue brings me closer, closer, closer to another release.

He growls as he licks up our combined juices. It's so dirty, so fucking filthy. And that only turns me on more. Weston spears his tongue into my entrance, massaging my walls and driving me insane.

My thighs snap around his head when he turns his attention to my clit, sucking on the over sensitized bundle of nerves. I twist in his grip and bow my back off the bed, only to have him spread his hand out over my lower belly and push me back down onto the mattress. He keeps his hand there, creating a delicious pressure that radiates from my core.

I grab at the sheets as my orgasm claws at my insides, tearing its way out and wringing pleasure from every cell in my body. Weston growls into my pussy, never letting up, expertly using his tongue and teeth to keep me at my peak for so damn long.

I'm shaking and sweating and whimpering his name over and over, unable to escape the brutal bliss overwhelming me. I feel an intense, all-consuming pressure tugging at my lower belly. It's unlike anything I've ever experienced and I'm almost afraid of what's happening to me.

My hands tangle in Weston's hair, gripping and twisting the strands, needing him to anchor me here on earth.

Another, stronger, wild orgasm threatens to end me completely, even as my body is still reeling from my previous one. Every muscle draws up tight, my joints locking, my breath frozen in my lungs. Time stands still, waiting, watching as I surrender to the pleasure Weston is bringing me.

All at once, everything inside me unravels. I gush for him, an embarrassing amount of wetness leaving me, as I scream and thrash around almost violently.

"Christ," he grunts, lapping up every last drop. "Jesus Christ," he repeats, his breathing ragged. "You squirted all over me, baby. So fucking hot."

I can't do anything except whimper and melt into the mattress, all the strength draining from my body. I'm vaguely aware of Weston leaving the bed, hardly registering when he cleans me up with a damp washcloth.

The bed dips with his weight, though I still can't open my eyes. He drapes my limp body over his and I automatically curl up into his chest. Weston presses a kiss to the top of my head and tucks a blanket around us.

"You okay, sunshine?" he whispers.

"So good," I mumble, hardly recognizing my own voice. Weston chuckles and kisses my head again.

"Me too, sweetheart. Me too."

Silence surrounds us as our hearts find the same rhythm, beating as one.

"You didn't fail me," I whisper, remembering why I crawled into his lap and made love to him in the first place. "You gave me strength. You gave me confidence. You gave me something to fight for. Don't you see? You saved me."

"Shay..." his voice cracks with emotion, making me squeeze my arms around him. "I love you so much, sunshine. So much it hurts."

"I love you, too, Weston. It's crazy how much I love you."

Another silence passes between us, then Weston cups the side of my face, and guides my head up so I'm meeting his gaze. "We don't have to do the play tomorrow. Or ever. Everyone would understand if you're not up for it."

I tilt my head to the side and furrow my brow, unsure where the change of subject came from. I can see it's weighing heavy on his heart, though, and needs to be addressed. Truthfully, the thought never crossed my mind.

I take a moment to consider his words, as well as my options. "A few short months ago, I would have jumped at the chance to slink back into the shadows and avoid the spotlight," I begin, hoping to convey my thoughts clearly. "But now...well, now I don't want to let Sean steal anything away from me ever again, including all the hard work we've put into preparing for the play. I want to do it. I want to do it for me, to prove to myself I can still stand strong even after everything."

I can't quite place the look in his eyes. He stares at me for long moments, studying me, assessing my words, my heart, and my mind. Finally, he breaks the silence. "God, you're incredible."

He seals his declaration with a kiss, somehow both fierce and tender. Just like him. I sink back down into his embrace, sighing in sweet satisfaction as sleep carries us away.

***

I blow out a breath and wipe my sweaty palms on my dress. I told Weston last night I wanted to do this for me and I still do, but that doesn't mean I'm not shaking like a leaf and nervous as hell.

It's opening night, minutes before the curtain opens. I know every line by heart, hell, I *feel* every line with each beat. I try channeling Seneca's confidence, but something is missing. Something like...

"Sunshine," Weston says in his deep, soothing voice. He wraps his arms around me from behind and kisses the side of my neck. "How are you feeling?"

I turn around in his arms and give him a chaste kiss that's over too soon.

"I'm...good..." I say in the least convincing voice.

Weston just smiles and kisses my forehead. "Yeah, you really are."

I roll my eyes at his response, but can't help the smile spreading across my face.

"Curtain call in sixty seconds!" someone shouts from backstage before listing off the cast members appearing in the opening scene, including Weston and me.

Weston steps back, but takes my hand in his, squeezing gently. "Come on, baby. Act with me," he says with a cheeky grin. I return his smile and squeeze his hand right back, watching as he steps out on stage first.

He's brilliant, of course, delivering the first lines of dialogue and setting the scene. My heart hammers in my chest and my stomach rolls in uneasy waves as I wait for my cue. This is it. This is what we've been working toward for so many weeks. This is my moment to shine...or to hide in the shadows once again. My understudy is waiting in the wings in case I choke, which I feel is a real possibility.

Someone nudges me in the ribs and nods their head toward center stage, where my mark is. I take a deep breath, square my shoulders, and try to move my feet. Only they won't budge. Closing my eyes, I push the fear back down and breathe in the confidence and safety Weston has provided every single day I've known him.

I take my first tentative step on stage, followed by another and another. I know I shouldn't, but my head turns to the side, gazing out at the audience. Most of the crowd is covered in darkness, much like I want to be right now, but I can tell it's a full house.

My foot catches on something and I stumble forward, though I regain my balance before falling flat on my face. My body flushes with embarrassment, sweat beading my forehead. This was a mistake. What was I thinking? I'm no star, and I'm certainly no sunshine, like Weston always calls me.

I feel myself starting to panic, my breaths becoming choppy. I'm seconds away from sprinting backstage and letting my understudy take my place, but something prompts me to fix my gaze forward, away from the audience.

My eyes catch Weston's brilliant green ones, a feeling of warmth washing over me and pushing my anxiety back just enough to take another step forward. Weston smiles at me, pride radiating from his features. Why is he proud of me? I'm barely five feet onto the stage and already I'm messing up.

He doesn't seem to think so, however. No, the look he's giving me right now lets me know he's proud of me for showing up, for trying, for...just being me. That realization wraps itself around me, blanketing me and protecting me from my own self-doubt.

I lift my chin up, straighten my spine, and give Weston a scowl, just like Seneca is supposed to do in this scene. He winks at me so only I can see, then gets right back into character. God, I love this man with my whole heart. The twinkle in his eye lets me know he feels the exact same way.

Chapter 15

Weston

Shay was absolutely brilliant from beginning to end, even those first few tentative steps she took on stage. I could see the panic flooding her mind and controlling her actions when she walked out on stage, nearly stumbling when she looked at the crowd. I know it took everything in her to even show up and I was so damn proud of my sunshine for daring to put herself out there, knowing she might fail.

The moment she chose herself over her fear will forever be branded in my mind. My heart. My fucking soul. Shay's eyes found mine, seeking solace as waves of anxiety crashed into her. I held her gaze and watched in awe as she pushed back her fear and marched toward me, pride evident in every step.

Her hand finds mine, breaking into my thoughts. I lace our fingers together as the curtains open to reveal the full cast taking a bow. I should be looking forward at the audience currently giving us a standing ovation, but I can't tear my gaze away from Shay's gorgeous smile and sparkling brown eyes.

She peers at me over her shoulder, her golden-brown irises turning dark with heat and hunger. I bite back a groan and try not to get a hard-on right here on stage, but that look tells me everything I need to know. My girl is riding the high of her first performance and I know just how I want to celebrate.

After a second bow, the cast and crew head backstage, preparing to go out in the lobby for a meet and greet. Shay and I will have to be fashionably late.

I drag my sunshine down the hall, glancing back at her to make sure she wants this as much as I do. When she bites her bottom lip, my cock jerks, and a growl works its way out from the depths of me.

We burst into my dressing room and I spin her around, pressing her back against the closed door before crashing my lips down on hers.

Shay grabs my shirt and pulls me closer as she sucks on my tongue, welcoming my kiss and fighting me for control. Her confidence and passion are so damn sexy, even more so knowing that I had something to do with building her up.

"Need you," she pleads, her voice breathy and laced with an undeniable urgency.

I growl into her lips, biting and nipping at her before licking into her mouth. My hands slide up the dress she's wearing, pushing the fabric up as I feel every inch of her soft, porcelain skin. She moans and drags her hands down my chest, her fingers tugging at my belt and then working my button and zipper open. Shay grips my hard as fuck dick, pulling me out and pumping me roughly.

"Fuck," I groan, loving the fact that she's this needy, this turned on, and this desperate for me. The thought makes me grunt possessively as my hands find the little lacy scrap of fabric covering her pussy. I rip it off her body and swallow down her gasp, my fingers sliding through her folds.

Goddamn, she's *soaked* for me, her cream dripping over my fingers and pooling in my hand. I circle her clit, the hard little pearl throbbing and swollen. Her legs shake, and I swear she's about to come from that one touch.

Without wasting any time, I grip her thighs and lift her up, pressing her against the door as she wraps her legs around my hips and digs her fingers into my shoulders. I look directly into her lust-filled eyes as I slam my cock inside her greedy little cunt.

Shay sucks in a breath and bites her lips to contain her scream. She comes as soon as I hit the end of her. I growl and hold myself deep inside of her, feeling her orgasm from the inside out, wave after wave of ecstasy rippling from her core and dripping down my aching dick.

She buries her head into the side of my neck, panting and shaking and whimpering my name. It's more than I can take. I pull out of her pulsing, tight little pussy and push back inside, fucking her roughly, just like we both need.

"Weston...oh fuck, Weston...I-I-I'm..."

Holy shit, is she...

The goddess in my arms tangles her fingers in my hair and rips my head up, the sting shooting straight bliss to my cock, making it swell up and stretch her out even more. Shay rests her sweaty forehead on mine, her chest heaving with each ragged breath as pained whimpers and grunts leave her mouth with each brutal thrust I'm giving her.

"Come for me, baby," I growl.

My words unlock her orgasm, and Jesus, she comes so hard, shaking and sobbing out her release as her arms and legs squeeze me tightly. I grip her ass in both hands, holding her to me as I grind against her cunt and clit, keeping her right there, forcing her to feel it, feel me, feel every ounce of pleasure I'm giving her.

My balls are heavy with my pent-up orgasm, my dick throbbing and angry as fuck. But I want more. So much more. And I know exactly how I want it.

I set Shay down, her legs trembling much like the rest of her. She tilts her head up, peering at me through the fog of bliss surrounding her. I kiss her forehead, nose, and lips, allowing her to catch her breath.

And then I spin her around, pushing her forward so she has to brace herself with her hands on the door. I flip the skirt of her dress up and grip her cheeks, spreading her open for me so I can sink into her tight, wet little hole. With a feral roar, I snap my hips against her ass, stuffing her full of my thickness.

"S-s-so d-d-deep," Shay stutters out on a moan, her pussy contracting around me over and over.

I'm reduced to grunts and growls, tipping my head back and bouncing her off my dick. Every muscle in my body tenses and my balls draw up tight, my orgasm crawling down my spine and stealing the air from my lungs.

Sliding one arm beneath Shay's hips, I hold her still as I piston in and out of her. She claws at the door then balls her hand up in a fist and pounds it against the wood as she succumbs to a final, vicious orgasm.

I slide my hand further down her body, rubbing her clit in furious circles as my other hand grabs a fistful of her white-blonde hair. She soaks my shaft with her cum and shudders in my arms. I bury my face between her neck and shoulder, breathing her in, feeling her shiver and pulse around me as I finally let go.

My orgasm barrels through me, clutching my muscles and making me shake uncontrollably as I come harder than I ever have. I shoot my release deep inside her still-throbbing core, each rope of cum forcing its way out in blissful, torturous waves.

It lasts forever, and yet it will never be enough. I know I'll want this woman wrapped around me as often as possible, chasing our pleasure and taking each other to heights unknown.

But right now, we need to clean up and make ourselves presentable.

We both groan as I reluctantly pull out of her. I growl when I see our combined releases dripping down the insides of her thighs, resisting the urge to get on my knees and lick it up.

Shay leans against the door, pressing her forehead against the wood as she tries to control her breathing. I grab some tissues and clean myself up, getting my pants zipped up and my belt on before turning back to Shay. She's still leaning against the door, seemingly unable to move. I smirk, knowing I gave her so many orgasms she can barely function.

I gently clean her up as well, righting her dress and placing a kiss on the back of her neck. I slowly turn her around and gather her limp body into my arms, holding her close. Shay sighs and snuggles into my chest, bringing me more joy and contentment than I've ever known.

My fingers comb through her beautiful hair, then wrap around the back of her neck so I can tilt her head up. "We gotta go meet your adoring fans," I murmur before pressing my lips to her hairline and breathing in her sweet scent.

She pouts, which is fucking adorable, but then gives me a cheeky grin. "Are you worried about being upstaged, Mr. Haze?"

"Worried? Not in the least. I already know you're better than me in every single way," I tell her with a wink as I step back and take her hand.

"Mm...I don't know about that. You're pretty great at giving me orgasms."

I groan, remembering all of the times she came for me in the last few minutes. "You're pretty great at giving me orgasms too, sunshine."

She giggles and just like every other time, it hits me deep. She's it for me. My sweet, dirty, insatiable, brave sunshine.

We walk hand in hand out to the lobby. When the crowd of people surges forward, I tuck Shay into my side, not wanting her to be overwhelmed by the mob. She takes it all in stride, however, shaking hands and chatting with her adoring fans. She even steps away from me to go talk to an older woman in a wheelchair. I'm so damn proud of her.

People are talking to me as well and I go through the motions of listening, nodding, and accepting their empty praise. Shay and I steal glances at each other, both of us eager to get this over with so we can be alone again.

I notice Shay stiffen as she looks across the small lobby and I'm by her side in a second, wrapping my arm around her waist and pulling her into my side once more.

"What's wrong?" I whisper.

"My parents."

I let out a breath of relief, knowing it's not somehow Sean, coming back for another beating. But then I remember it's their fault for bringing him into her life in the first place. Anger wells up inside of me, my muscles tensing and preparing for a fight. Shay brushes her fingers across my chest, the light touch calming me down and grounding me once again.

Just in time, too. An older couple approaches us, reeking of old money and false pretenses.

"Well, well, well, Weston Cooper Haze," her dad says, clapping a hand over my shoulder as if we're friends who haven't seen each other in a while.

"Mr. Sullivan," I respond curtly, twisting away from his grip.

"What brings you to this...humble little theater?" I grit my teeth, hating his condescending tone. Neither one of them has even acknowledged Shay. If I didn't already loathe them, that would have done it.

"Needed a change of scenery," I mutter, tucking Shay further into my side as if I can shield her from her cold parents.

I see Mrs. Sullivan's gaze drop to where my hand is resting on Shay's hip, holding her close. Her eyes go wide with surprise and then dark with greed. I'm all too familiar with that look. It's pathetic how transparent and shallow these two are.

"Shay, dear, you didn't say you were working with Weston Cooper Haze for your little play. Why don't you two come over for dinner tonight? I'll have the cook—"

"We have plans," I grunt, cutting her off. Normally when meeting the parents of the love of your life, I'd imagine you'd want to make a good impression. But her parents lost my respect far before I ever laid eyes on them and this meeting only solidifies that fact.

"Tomorrow, then?" Mr. Sullivan prompts, now getting the hint that Shay and I are together. I can see him already planning a pitch for me to invest in his company or whatever the fuck he does.

"No," I growl, causing the pair of them to gasp and step back a bit.

"Shay?" her mother questions, looking at her daughter for the first time since coming over here.

"You heard him," she answers with all the confidence in the world. Damn, today is such a big day for my sunshine, and I'm the lucky bastard who gets to be here for all of her accomplishments. "We're booked tomorrow night. And the next night, right, Weston?"

She turns and looks at me, a playful, knowing grin on her lips. God, I love her so much.

"That's right, sunshine. In fact, I think our schedule is full for the foreseeable future." Without another word, I spin us around and walk away, leaving Mr. and Mrs. Sullivan gaping after us. I can't help myself. I look at them over my shoulder and say, "I'll have my people call your people."

"Yeah," Shay giggles. "Don't call us, we'll call you."

She gives me another sexy smirk, forcing me to stop and kiss it off her lips. "Ready to get out of here?" I murmur.

"Not so fast," a familiar voice sounds from behind me. "Aren't you going to introduce me to the lovely lady who tamed your wild ass?"

I look over at Ted, the annoyance dropping from my features at the interruption. It's good to see him and I truly do want these two to meet.

"This is my Shay," I say with a goofy-ass grin on my face. I can't help it when I'm around her.

"Hi," she squeaks out before clearing her throat and trying again. "Nice to meet you...?"

"Ted," he answers. "I'm this kid's agent, at least for now." Shay shakes his hand and peers over at me, the question clear in her eyes. I'll have time to address that later. "Are you looking for an agent? Your performance was incredible. Was that really your first time on stage?"

Shay blushes at the compliment and nods, thanking him. I watch her and Ted chat, though she turns down his offer to move to LA and take my place as his star client. An unnamable emotion clogs my throat as I watch the two most important people in my life laughing, even if it's at my expense.

My hand finds the small of Shay's back, rubbing light circles there. As much as I love Ted and I love that he and Shay seem to be fast friends, I need to get my girl home. I have plans for us tonight. Plans that can't wait another second.

"Breakfast tomorrow, Ted?" I cut in, my voice rougher than I intended. He gives me a sly smirk, knowing exactly what I'm up to.

"Of course," he responds easily. Ted nods slightly, the twinkle in his eye letting me know he approves of my Shay and my life choices.

"Perfect!" Shay says excitedly. "It was really nice to meet—hey!" Shay gasps as I bend down and throw her over my shoulder, unable to wait any longer. Ted chuckles while Shay tries to sound indignant. "What do you think you're doing?" There's laughter threaded through her words that lets me know she's not that upset about the turn of events.

"I've got a surprise for you," I say with a shrug, storming backstage, not caring who sees us.

"I don't have any panties," she whispers, a bit of nervousness creeping into her voice.

"You don't need them for what I have in mind."

Shay pounds her little fists on my back, making me laugh. "I mean, you've got me slung over your shoulder in just a dress!" she hisses.

I pat her ass and tighten my grip around her thighs. "I'm not worried about it."

Shay scoffs and mutters "caveman" under her breath before bursting into giggles.

After a quick stop in each of our dressing rooms to gather our things, I help Shay into my car and buckle her seatbelt. She sighs dreamily, and I have to kiss her lips. It's a necessity.

"Where are we going? Isn't your place the other way?"

"I said I had a surprise, didn't I?"

"I thought you meant a sexy surprise," she mumbles. Is she pouting again? I'm tempted to pull the car over and suck on that bottom lip before kissing her soundly, but I manage to stay the course.

"There will be plenty of sexy surprises later," I promise, taking her hand in mine as we drive through the city. Shay squirms in her seat, making me groan.

A few minutes later, we pull up to a beautiful craftsman style house nestled in the affluent but charming neighborhood of Queen Anne.

"Oh, wow," Shay breathes out, her eyes going wide as she takes in the handcrafted details on the outside, including the wrap-around porch. "Where are we?"

"Home."

"What? What are you talking about?"

Instead of answering her, I get out of the car, helping her out as well. I pull her along, up the stairs, until we're standing in front of the door. Her eyes go wide in shock as I take out a key and unlock the door, ushering her inside. Standing behind her, I wrap my arms around her waist and pull her into my chest, holding her while she looks all around.

"What do you think?" I finally ask after a few moments of silence.

"You're going to live here? You're staying?"

I turn her around so we're facing each other, then I cup her cheeks and meet her gaze. "I was hoping you'd stay here with me," I murmur, trying to gauge her reaction.

Her eyes well up with tears, but the soft smile on her lips tells me they are happy tears. I hope.

"You... want me to... live with you?"

"Well, I'm hoping you'll marry me, but we'll take things slow."

"Moving in after knowing each other for two months isn't exactly slow. Wait, hold up, did you say *marry you*?"

"Yup," I confirm. "And one day have my children, but like I said, we can take things slow."

I grin as I watch her sputter in disbelief. I know she wants this as much as I do. I feel it in every kiss, every smile, every heated gaze, and contented sigh. Now I just need to get her to admit it.

"Children?" she squeaks out.

"I'm hoping for at least three, but I'm up for negotiating. Come on, let's take the tour."

I tug a still shocked Shay along, giving her time to digest everything I've said so far. The house is still empty—I just closed on it last week, after all, but I can't wait to let Shay go crazy and decorate it however she wants. All I want is for her to fill it with her light. Everything else is just the icing on top.

We end the tour in the kitchen, which is even bigger and more impressive than the one in the penthouse I've been staying in. Shay still hasn't said anything, but I've got one more card up my sleeve. I knew the house would be a lot for her to take in, so I wanted to remind her that we're still us, no matter where we live.

There's a tray set up on the kitchen counter with a silver dome covering it, just like I requested. Ted really is the best agent ever, calling in some last-minute favors and pulling strings behind the scenes. He was more than thrilled to have a hand in all of this.

I walk over to the counter and pull the lid off, revealing two bowls of tomato soup and a stack of grilled cheese sandwiches. Shay gasps, her hands covering her mouth as tears stream down her face.

"These aren't going to be nearly as good as the ones you made me, but I hear Purple doesn't suck when it comes to making food."

This earns me a watery smile and a stuttered out laugh. "Weston..."

I pull her into my arms, wrapping her up in my embrace and kissing the top of her head. "You captured my attention the moment I saw you," I whisper. "And with each passing day, you captured my heart. I know that sounds cheesy, but—"

"It's perfect," she murmurs, lifting her head up and kissing my chin. "I want this. I want you. I want the life you've shown me. It's crazy though, right?"

"It's perfect." I echo her words, resting my forehead against hers. "And crazy. And exciting. And so damn real. I'm all in, sunshine. All you have to do is say yes."

She stares at me in silence and for the first time, I worry I pushed her too far, too fast. Doubt creeps in, but before I spiral downward, my Shay saves me.

"Yes," she whispers onto my lips. "Yes, yes, yes, a million times, yes." Shay giggles at her cliché answer and I hold her closer, feeling her laughter as it rolls through her body.

"Are you reusing old lines on me, sunshine?" I growl playfully into the side of her neck.

"Who, me?"

"Yes, you." I cut off her response with an all-consuming kiss, tasting promises of forever on her tongue. "I love you so much, Shay. With everything I am."

"I love you, too." I'll never get tired of hearing those words from her. "Now, where's my ring?"

I bark out a laugh. I'll never get tired of her sassy mouth, either.

"Is the house not enough for you?" I tease.

"It's nice and all, but diamonds are a girl's best friend."

I smack her ass playfully, making her jump back as a cute little growl falls from her lips. "Will this do?" I take the little velvet box from my pocket and flip the lid open, showing her the diamond ring I picked up last week, the same day I closed on the house.

Shay nods her head furiously, making me chuckle. I go to slip it on her finger, but she pulls her hand away. "You didn't get down on one knee."

"I didn't want to be too cliché for you."

That grin returns in full force as she offers me her hand once more. My sweet girl stares at her new piece of jewelry with tears in her eyes. I lift her hand up to my lips and kiss her ring, and then kiss her soft, pliant lips.

"Is this for real?" she whispers.

"It's for real. It's forever. It's you and me, sunshine. And that's no line."

Shay giggles through her tears and melts into my embrace. "You and me," she whispers back.

We hold each other for God knows how long, sharing the same breath, feeling the weight of this moment. The moment our happily ever after begins.

Epilogue

Shay

"That's a wrap!" I announce as I carry a tray of cookies and other goodies down the aisle of the theater.

"Are you stealing my lines now, sunshine?" Weston asks once I'm standing next to him in the front row.

"I can't let you have all the fun, can I?" I try to give him a sly smirk, but it turns into a cheesy grin, much like it always does when I'm around Weston. I can't help it. The man makes me so damn happy every single day.

He returns my smile and sets the tray of treats down on the folding table in front of us before wrapping an arm around me. Weston tucks me into his side and gives some stage directions to the high school kids currently rehearsing on stage.

I melt into his side and peer up at him, loving the sense of pride and purpose I find there. I watch him watching the kids, taking in his slightly furrowed brow, strong nose, and soft lips, curved up on one end.

We opened the SJ Haze theater nearly four years ago now—a year after we were married. We hold indie productions, rent out the space, feature up and coming directors and theater companies, as well as offer acting classes for underprivileged kids, like the one I'm currently interrupting. Sometimes Weston and I make an appearance in the performances, but mostly we're content to provide a space for actors and directors to cut their teeth.

"Sara, can you say that last line again? Don't look at the script. Close your eyes and just imagine what your character would feel. Don't worry about the words so much as the emotion you're conveying. Make sense?"

Sara nods her head and looks at the script one more time before closing her eyes. Weston and I watch as she stutters out a few words, probably trying to remember them just right. And then it happens. The proverbial lightbulb flickers and then shines brightly as Sara delivers her lines with such overwhelming emotion I'm brought to tears. I recognize her monologue. It's the same one I gave for my audition all those years ago.

"Baby, what's wrong?" Weston whispers.

"It's just... it's beautiful, you know?"

He gives me a soft smile and nods. "I do know. I watched you do the very same thing when you first walked out on stage for your audition. I saw the moment everything changed."

I lean my head against his chest and let him hold me while we watch Sara and Nathan get into the scene. Nathan is still holding back, not able to fully let go of the awkwardness of being on stage, but Sara is doing her best to show him it's okay.

Nathan grumbles something and then sighs in frustration, running his hands through his hair.

"What's going on, Nate?" Weston asks in his calming, understanding voice.

"Nothing. I just...I don't know. I can't visualize it like you tell us to."

"That's alright. Sometimes that happens when you've got a lot of other things on your mind. Anything you want to talk about?"

"No, just tired, I guess. Can we take a break? Are those cookies?" His eyes have a slightly devious sparkle to them, letting both Weston and I know that was his plan all along.

"We'll take a break soon," Weston answers. "But first...let's show 'em how it's done, sunshine." He grins at me and tugs me along, hopping on stage before helping me up as well. Weston twirls me around in his arms, making me giggle, before bending me backward. "Come on, baby. Act with me," he whispers onto my lips.

Before I can respond, he stands up and twirls me away, letting go of my hand so we're standing face to face. We don't need the script; we both know the lines by heart.

"I'm no damsel in distress, and if I am, I'll be my own white knight. I refuse to become that girl again, the one who wilted and withered away, silently decaying behind closed doors. Do I want love? Yes, but on my own terms. I'm not a kept woman. Not anymore. I want a partner, a protector, a friend. I want a lover. But more than that I want to be respected and seen for who I am. I want someone to challenge me as much as they cherish me. I want it all. And I won't settle for anything less. Are you that man? Will you give me everything?"

Weston looks at me with such overwhelming pride and reverence, his green eyes even misting over with a few tears. He takes a step closer to me, and then another, his hand coming up to cup the side of my face.

"Everything. All of me. I'll be whatever you need. Protector, best friend, supporter. Lover." His easy smile turns serious, his eyes begging me to believe him. There's such longing there, such truth and vulnerability. "I love you."

With that, his lips meet mine, fulfilling all of the promises he just made. I'm vaguely aware of the students cat-calling, sighing, or making gagging noises, but right now, Weston is all that matters.

"It was never an act with you," I murmur once we break apart.

"Sunshine, you were the only real thing in my life."

Of course, I have to kiss him again after a line like that. He smiles against my lips and snakes one hand up my back, only to dip me low and kiss down my neck. I giggle and squirm away from him, knowing we're giving the kids a show. Weston loops his arm around my waist and tucks me into his side, pressing a kiss to the top of my head.

We watch the students hop off stage and grab the snacks I laid out for them. The whole time, I'm cradled in my husband's warm embrace, my ear pressed against his chest, right over his heart. Like always, the strong, steady beat grounds me and brings me peace.

"Love you," I whisper.

"Love you so damn much, Shay. You're the light of my life." I giggle and roll my eyes at his cheesy line. "What? It's true. You're my sunshine."

I smile at him and snuggle back into his arms, letting him hold me and rock me back and forth. I might be his sunshine, but he's the one who brought me out of the shadows.

Connect with me!

Check out my website, cameronhart.net[1], for sneak previews on my latest projects.

Follow me on social media:

Facebook Page - facebook.com/cameronhartauthor
Instagram - instagram.com/cameron.hart.author
TikTok - tiktok.com/@author.cameron.hart
Goodreads - goodreads.com/16081533.Cameron_Hart
Bookbub - bookbub.com/authors/cameron-hart

---

1. https://cameronhart.net/